Katherine Garbera is the *USA Today* bestselling author of more than forty books. She's always believed in happy endings and lives in Southern California with her husband, children and their pampered pet, Godiva. Visit Katherine on the web at www.katherinegarbera. com, or catch up with her on Facebook and Twitter.

This book is dedicated to my sister Linda for always having my back. I love you, Linda.

One

"Go ahead and look, Macy, you are even more beautiful than before," Dr. Justin Webb said.

Macy Reynolds held the mirror loosely in her left hand and slowly lifted it so she could see her face, but she closed her eyes at the last second before she could catch a glimpse. Three years ago she'd been beautiful. She'd even been crowned the Rose Queen of Royal, Texas, as an eighteen-year-old girl. But all that had changed in one fateful car accident. She'd lost her looks, her man and her confidence.

This had supposedly been the last surgery she'd need, but her looks, which she'd once taken for granted, were now the bane of her existence. She was never going to be that beautiful girl again.

Dr. Webb put his hand on her shoulder. "Trust me, Macy."

She wasn't sure she trusted any man but her daddy. He'd stood by her through everything.

Macy and Harrison were all each other had, but she knew she couldn't spend the rest of her life sitting in Dr. Webb's office with her eyes closed.

She thought of the courageous kids in the Burn Unit at this hospital where she volunteered. They weren't afraid to look in the mirror and she shouldn't be either.

She opened one eye and then, surprised by her reflection, she opened the other. Her skin was pale and flawless, the way it used to be. No scars marred the surface. Her pixie nose had been restored to its former shape; she reached up and touched it. Her eyes hadn't been injured in the car accident and her clear green gaze remained the same.

Her lips were the only thing that were really different. A piece of glass had cut her upper lip and now she had a tiny indentation where there used to be none.

"Thank you, Dr. Webb," she said. Still not perfect, but at least she was done with surgeries.

"See. I was right, you are more beautiful than before," he said.

She just smiled and nodded. She put the mirror facedown on the bed next to her. "Don't take this the wrong way, Doc, but I'll be glad not to have to see you again."

Dr. Webb laughed. "Me too, Macy. I'll send the nurse in with some paperwork and then you will be free to go."

He started to leave, but she called him back. "Thank you, Dr. Webb. All your hard work has really made a difference to me."

"You are very welcome," he said and then left.

Her cell phone vibrated as she received a text message and she glanced down at it. The message was from her dad.

How did everything go at the doctor's?

Macy thought about her looks, but she knew she was so much more than just a pretty face now. And Dr. Webb had been a miracle worker to get her face this close to how she'd looked before the accident. She was never going to be exactly the same, but Dr. Webb had done a really good job.

Just fine, Daddy.

I bet you look better than fine. I'll see you when you get home tonight.

Yes. See you then.

Love you, baby girl.

Love you, Daddy.

She and her father were closer now than ever. After her fiancé, Benjamin, left her while she was in the hospital, she'd had no choice but to lean—and lean hard—on her father. The accident had taken everything from her.

But now she was back to her old self. Or at least she really hoped she was. She was ready to stand on her own and she knew she had to get out of her daddy's safe little world and back to her own.

She finished up with the nurse and left the office. And for the first time since then she didn't immediately put on the large sunglasses that covered half her face.

She opened the lobby door and walked right into a man. He caught her shoulders as she tottered on her heels and almost fell over.

"Thank you," she said, looking up into the bluest eyes she'd ever seen. Christopher Richardson…her high school sweetheart and the man she'd broken up with when her daddy had demanded it.

It had been almost fourteen years since they'd last seen each other and she…well, she felt as if no time had passed. Chris looked just as handsome as he had in high school and just as tempting.

"Macy. Some things never change and you get more beautiful each time I see you," he said. There was more than a hint of irony in his voice.

She flushed, remembering how she'd dumped him all those years ago. "You haven't seen me since high school."

"True enough. When a woman tells me to hit the road I tend to do that and not look back," he said. "What are you doing here?"

Should she apologize for what she'd done years earlier? She knew that she owed him way more than a casual "I'm sorry" though. "Um…I had an accident a few years ago," she said. Dang it, why hadn't she lied and said she was here for her charitable work with the Burn Unit.

"I heard about that. Are you okay now?"

She nodded. "Better every day."

"And you, Mr. Big City, what brings you back to Royal?"

"My mom is in the hospital. But I'm back in Royal to bid on rebuilding the Texas Cattleman's Club headquarters."

"Oh. I think I heard something about how you're in real estate like my father," she said.

"I'm bigger than your father, Macy. In fact, Richardson Development is the biggest developer in Texas."

"Wow," she said. She didn't know how to respond. Did he think that she'd be impressed—that she still measured people by their bank accounts?

So she changed the subject. "I hope your mom is okay," Macy said.

She remembered Margaret Richardson as a very kind woman who thought Chris hung the moon.

"She'll be fine. She has a recurring heart problem but the doctors are taking good care of her," Chris said.

An awkward silence lagged between them. He was standing there in front of her looking very sexy and she felt bruised and battered.

"Where are you living now?" Chris asked at last.

"With my dad on our ranch." It had been a hard time when she'd had the accident, and moving back to the ranch had been her only option.

"I never suspected you'd stay with your daddy, but I guess that makes sense," Chris said.

"I moved back to town a little while ago," she said. She didn't have to justify her choices to anyone, but Chris made her feel as if she should explain.

"Go figure. I guess I always thought you'd find a nice rich boy and settle down," Chris said. He rubbed a hand through his shaggy blond hair and gave her that charming grin of his that made her want to melt.

"I did. But he ran away when I proved not to be

the Texas beauty queen he'd hoped for," she said, and thought she didn't sound bitter at all.

"Loser," Chris said.

She laughed. "He was a very respectable man from a good family."

"If he couldn't make you happy then he's a loser. I always loved your spirit."

"Why, thank you, Chris. I think you are just what the doctor ordered."

"While I'm here, I could use the insight of someone who's been living here. Maybe you can tell me a little about what's going on at the club. Would you join me for dinner tonight?"

She thought about it for a minute, but she knew she wanted to go. "I will. If you're lucky I will introduce you to the next president of TCC, Ms. Abigail Langley."

"I'd heard all the wives and daughters were campaigning for Abby. That's the kind of information I need before I put in my bid to do the development," Chris said.

"We are. It's about time women had an equal stake in the Texas Cattleman's Club. My father and his cronies aren't sure what they are going to do. It completely threw them when Abby's husband died and for the first time since Tex Langley founded the club a hundred years ago they didn't have a male-Langley heir as a member. That's the only reason Abby's an honorary member."

"That's not my fight. I'm just the developer they're thinking of hiring. What do you say to six-thirty? If you're staying with your dad, I have the address."

"Sounds perfect. I'll see you then."

Macy walked away very aware that Chris was watching her. The confidence she lost when Benjamin left her was finally coming back. She wanted to pretend that it was because the last of her surgeries was over, but she knew that it was because of Chris.

Chris Richardson had been on the high school varsity football team, which had made him something akin to a god in the tiny town of Royal, Texas. And it hadn't taken Macy too long to set her sights on him. She was used to getting what she'd wanted back then, so he was hers just as junior year ended. They dated over the summer and through homecoming, but then her father had put his foot down.

Harrison Reynolds didn't want his daughter dating a boy whose dad worked for the oil companies instead of owning one. A man who wasn't a member of the Texas Cattleman's Club, ensuring his son would never be one either.

Looking back now, Macy wished she'd been a different sort of girl and had maybe stood up for Chris. But she hadn't been and she wondered sometimes if the accident was what it had taken to really shake things up for her.

One thing she knew for sure was that she'd never really gotten over him and she was glad he was back in Royal.

Chris watched Macy walk away. The sway of her hips and those gorgeous legs going a long way toward reminding him why he'd gone after her in high school. It hadn't mattered to Macy's dad that he was a star wide receiver back then, because he came from the wrong side of town.

But today he was here to visit his mom and to do

a little work on the Texas Cattleman's Club project. It was one of the most exclusive luxury country clubs in Texas. Only families with the right pedigree and the right amount of money could get in. And Chris's working-class dad hadn't provided either for Chris; though today he had more than enough money to buy himself a place in Royal's exclusive club.

He took the elevator to the sixth floor and asked at the reception desk for his mom's room. He walked down the hall to her room and opened the door to see her sitting up in her bed watching TV.

"Hi, Mom."

"Chris! I didn't think you were ever going to get here," she said.

She fumbled around for the remote, but he was at her side before she found it. He leaned down to give her a big bear hug and a kiss. Then handed her the remote. She muted the television, which had been at high volume. Her hearing wasn't as good as it used to be.

"This is extreme, Mom, even for you. Falling down so I'd come and visit you. You knew I'd be here on Texas Cattleman's Club business this weekend."

She shook her head and smiled at him. "I guess the good Lord thought I needed to see you before then. What took you so long to get up here?"

"I ran into Macy Reynolds."

His mom sat up a little straighter. It had never sat right with her that Macy had dumped him just before the senior prom.

"What did you say to her?" Maggie asked.

"Just chitchat. I'm having dinner with her tonight," Chris said. He tried hard to sound casual, but this was his mother and she knew him better than anyone else in the world.

"Is that wise?"

He shrugged. "I have no idea. But it will definitely be fun. She's changed."

"I heard about the accident," Maggie said.

"What happened?" Chris asked as he pulled a chair up close to his mom's bed. She had the same thick blondish hair he did, but she wore hers straight. It hung around her pretty face in a fashionable style. Her eyes were blue like his, but she had a pert little nose and a full bow mouth.

"It was all over the news. Her little BMW convertible was hit from behind in traffic and her car slammed into an eighteen-wheeler. The car was engulfed in flames. She's lucky to be alive. But horribly scarred. At least that's what I heard down at the Royal Diner."

"That place is a hotbed for gossip, but it doesn't mean that any of that is true," Chris said. The diner had the best greasy food in West Texas, but some of the stories to come out of there weren't always the whole truth.

"It was real enough. She had to move back in with Harrison and has spent the past few years having a series of surgeries. It was heartbreaking, Chris, to see that pretty girl in bandages. She couldn't walk for the first six months."

Chris felt weak in the stomach at the thought of Macy in so much pain. He shook his head. "She seems much better now."

"I think she is," Maggie said. "But what about you? Tell me about your work with the Texas Cattleman's Club."

"There isn't much to tell right now, Mom. I'm going

to meet with Brad Price and then start working on my bid to develop and build a new headquarters for the Cattleman's Club. I have a basic idea of what they want, but that's it."

"Are you going out there today?" Maggie asked.

"Yes, I am. I've been granted full privileges to the club while I'm working on the project."

"Where are you staying?" she asked.

"With you. I think you might need someone at home with you when you get out of the hospital. Plus, the doctors still can't figure out why you have these episodes," he said with a grin.

"Good. You don't have to stay with me, but I'm glad for the company. I miss you, Chris."

He stood up and smiled down at his mom. Her face so familiar and dear to him, he brushed a kiss over her forehead and then tucked the covers more closely around her body. "I've missed you too, Mom."

He chatted with her for a few more minutes but then had to leave. He was due to meet Brad. Brad was determined to be the next president of the Texas Cattleman's Club and, given his background as the son of one of Royal's banking families, most people thought he was a shoo-in to win. Chris wanted to take a look at the existing buildings and the property so he knew exactly what he was working with on this project. Everyone who'd grown up in Royal was aware of the club, but Chris wanted to get up to speed on the details of the property.

"I'll stop by tonight before my dinner date," he said to his mom.

"Perfect. Good luck with your business," Maggie said.

Chris left with the impression that his mother had

no idea how successful he was at what he did. But that didn't bother him. He was really only interested in making sure that Macy and Harrison knew how successful he was. And before he went back to Dallas, the Reynoldses definitely would.

As soon as he stepped out of the hospital he was reminded it was August in West Texas and hot as Hades. He loosened his tie and pulled out a pair of sunglasses and hit the remote start button on his Range Rover HSE. He was having his Porsche transported to Royal so he could use that while he was in town.

He wanted the locals to know that Chris Richardson was back and he had plenty of money this time. He may not be a full-fledged member of the Texas Cattleman's Club, but he took a lot of pride in knowing that he had enough money in his bank accounts to be one if he pushed.

He wondered what kind of car Macy drove. He should have asked a few more questions about her accident. It was hard for him to imagine the girl he'd known, who'd lived a decidedly charmed life, having to go through that kind of painful recovery. But then life seldom turned out the way that most people thought it would. Chris had proved that by making a success of himself in the same field as Harrison Reynolds. And tonight he'd be sitting in the dining room of the Texas Cattleman's Club with Macy. Life was sweet.

Macy couldn't stop looking at herself in the mirror and she knew that was a recipe for disaster, so she forced herself away from it and back to her computer. She had a lot of work to get done before her dinner with Chris.

Chris Richardson. Dang, she'd never expected to see him again. She wished she could say that the years hadn't been good to him, but they had. If he'd developed a beer belly and lost some of his hair maybe she wouldn't be quivering in anticipation waiting for six-thirty to roll around.

The doorbell rang and Macy sat up a little straighter, leaving her home office. She heard Jessie, her dad's housekeeper, talking to someone. Macy rose from her chair, and went out into the hallway. She smiled at Abigail Langley.

Abby and Macy went way back to high school, but they had really become closer after Macy's accident when Abby had become her rock. Then last year, unexpectedly, Abby's husband had died of a brain aneurysm and Macy had had a chance to return the favor.

Abby had long wavy red hair and bright blue eyes. She was pretty and tall and walked into the room as if she owned it. Macy envied her friend that confidence. She'd thought the surgeries that restored her looks and her ability to walk would be enough, but this afternoon she'd realized they weren't.

"Hi, there, Abby," Macy said.

"Hello, gorgeous! You look wonderful. No need to ask how the doctor's appointment went."

Macy flushed. "I still don't look like me."

Abby wrapped her arm around Macy's shoulder. "Yes, you do. This is the new you."

"You are right. So…guess who I ran into at the hospital?" Macy asked as she led Abby into the den. The room was richly appointed with deep walnut paneling and oversize leather couches and chairs. This was where her father hosted football parties for his college buddies and where, when Macy had turned sixteen, she'd hosted her first boy-girl party.

On the wall was a portrait of her that her father had commissioned when she was eighteen, and Macy took a seat that deliberately kept her back to the picture. She hated looking at old pictures of herself. She didn't like being reminded of who she used to be.

"Christopher Richardson," Abby said with a twinkle in her eye.

"How did you know?"

"I have my sources. What did he say?"

"Nothing much. We're going to dinner tonight so I can catch him up on all the gossip about the club. He's in town to consult on developing the new clubhouse."

"Well, that's news to me. I'm going to have to have a little discussion with Mr. Bradford Price."

"I wasn't sure if you knew about it or not," Macy confessed. Abby was rumored to be the descendant of infamous Texas outlaw Jessamine Golden and was making history herself as the first female member of the Texas Cattleman's Club.

Abby and Macy had bonded over their shared tragedies. When Macy had been so badly injured and struggling to recover, Abby had been there for her, something Macy would never forget.

Abby didn't say anything else, and Macy was a little worried about her friend. She suspected that Abby was using the connection and campaign to become the next president of the club to distract herself from the fact that Richard was really gone.

"Whose house are we placing the flamingos at next?"

"Mrs. Doubletree has been selected, but we are going to hit TCC first."

"Great. What time and when?"

"Tonight, but if you can't make it due to your dinner date, I will understand. In fact, I think we might be moving them while you are dining. You can help out the next time."

Macy hated to miss out on helping Abby with the flamingos. Since she'd been so badly scarred and had frequently had bandages on to help her healing body stay infection free for the past three years, helping place pink flamingos in the yards of wealthy community members under cover of night had been the only thing she'd really felt comfortable doing to help out.

They placed the flamingos in the yards of different community members, and then the recipient of the flamingoes paid at least ten dollars a bird to have them relocated to another yard. The money was being raised for Helping Hands, a women's shelter run by Summer Franklin in nearby Somerset.

Macy had always been big into causes, having been on the board of the Reynolds Charitable Trust since she turned twenty-one. But normally she just wrote checks and organized galas. Actually getting out and doing things was new to her.

"I will try to make it. It's the only thing I've really been able to do to help," Macy said.

"You've done more than that," Abby said. "You've been helping me out a lot with my campaign."

"I think it's about time that the Texas Cattlemen had some women in their ranks. The shake-up last year helped change it from Daddy's stuffy old men's club into something that our generation can really be a part of."

"I agree. And when I become president of the club, that's not the only change we will be making."

"Good to hear it," Macy said. She and Abby chatted a few minutes longer before Abby had to leave.

After her friend's departure, Macy went upstairs and had a long bath. She didn't want to be nervous about tonight, but it was the first date she'd been on since her fiancé had left her. And that made it important.

She thought about her scarred body and how she still felt like the mess she'd been after that first surgery. She didn't want to stare at herself in the mirror, but her psychiatrist said that she had to accept what she looked like now if she was ever going to move on.

She let the towel drop and stood in front of the mirror, letting her gaze drift down her own body. She saw the scarring on her right side, then the muscle she'd lost on her inner thigh.

She felt tears stir in her eyes and she bit her lower lip. Her body wasn't going to get any better. This was how she'd always look. She glanced back at her face and for a moment almost resented the fact that her face was back to "normal" because the rest of her wasn't. Not even inside was she the same woman she used to be.

She didn't dwell on the fact that the date was with Christopher Richardson. He'd been her first love and she wasn't sure she'd ever really gotten over him. She'd been young and impetuous when they'd met and he'd been forbidden fruit. She'd wanted him because her father hadn't wanted her to have him. It wasn't lost on her that she'd used him and now she was going to have to apologize. The girl she'd been pre-accident would have handled it with her normal panache, but Macy wasn't that woman anymore and she suddenly dreaded the coming evening.

Two

Macy had driven herself to the Texas Cattleman's Club because she was meeting Abby later to move the flamingos. But also because she didn't want to be too dependent on Chris getting her home. The dining room was traditional Texas with lots of big heavy dark wood pieces and portraits of the founding members on the walls.

She went to the bar area and ordered a glass of Chardonnay while she waited for Chris. She hated being alone in a public place. It didn't matter that she'd grown up coming to this club. She felt so exposed because of her accident.

She felt as if everyone was watching her and whispering behind her back. She knew it was her imagination. But Royal was a town that was given to gossip and she hated to be fodder for it. When she'd been younger—before her accident—she'd tried to do daring things to make people notice her, but now she just longed to be invisible.

"Macy?"

She glanced toward the end of the bar where her father stood with one of his business partners. Her dad was one of the old guard at the club. But he was fighting to remain loyal after the scandal involving Sebastian Hunter a few years ago. His friend's embezzlement had shaken him. Sebastian had tried to sabotage the very club he'd been a member of.

"Hello, Dad," she said, turning to give him a kiss when he approached.

He lifted her chin and she knew he was looking for the scar that used to run the length of the left side of her face. Her dad had been the first one to see her after the accident. Her fiancé, Benjamin, didn't think he could handle seeing her that way. So her father had come in and held her hand and told her that she was still his princess.

"Beautiful," he said. He kissed her forehead.

She blinked back tears. "Thanks, Daddy."

He handed her a handkerchief. Then pulled her close for a hug. She hid her face in his shoulder the way she used to when she was little and didn't want to face something.

"What are you doing up here, Mace? Did I forget a dinner date for tonight?" Harrison asked.

"Actually, no. I'm meeting someone," she said. She had no idea how he'd take the news that she was having dinner with Chris. So she decided to keep his name to herself. Chris had certainly changed since high school, but tonight she wanted the fairy tale. She'd felt like the Beast locked away for so long. Now she wanted to feel attractive and to enjoy being out on a date with a good-looking guy. She and Chris Richardson had always made a stunning couple.

"That's good. I wanted to take you out to celebrate the removal of the last bandages, but you know how it is with work. I don't keep banker's hours." She and her dad had been alone since her mother had died when Macy was a toddler. They celebrated things in their own way and on their own time. She knew he'd make it up to her.

"You never have," she said. Macy was very aware of how hard her father worked. He owned one of the largest construction companies in Texas. And flew from Royal to other parts of the state most weeks. He also had his weekly poker game in Midland and a twice-yearly fishing trip with his college buddies.

The waiter called his name and he hesitated. "Do you want me to wait with you?"

She smiled at him. "No, I'm fine. Go on. I'll see you at breakfast tomorrow."

He hugged her quickly and then walked away. She turned back to the bar just as her wine arrived. She took a sip before glancing around the bar. Chris waved at her as he walked toward her.

"Sorry if I kept you waiting," Chris said. "I'll have a Lone Star beer," he told the bartender.

"Right away, sir," the man said.

"You didn't. I was a little early. Since the accident I...I drive a little more slowly," she said. There really wasn't any part of her life that hadn't been affected by it.

"You will have to tell me more about what happened.

Mom knew some of the details," he said. "Let's grab a booth while we wait to be seated for dinner."

She nodded and he led the way to one of the small intimate booths in the corner. Macy slid in and then waited while Chris did the same. He sat directly across from her and put his elbows on the table.

"So what happened? Mom said you'd been burned," he said.

She shrugged. "No one's really ever asked me about it before, because it was on the news."

"Not in Dallas," he said. "But then most of the stuff that happens here doesn't make the headlines there."

"I don't know what to say except my car was hit by a long-haul trucker and that it was a mangled mess... all the rescuers said I was lucky to be alive."

She held her hands loosely together, taking off the ring on her right hand and playing with it before putting it back on. She didn't like to talk about the accident. To be honest, she remembered so little of it.

"I'm glad that you are such a lucky woman, Macy," he said.

The bartender arrived with his beer. She studied him as he took a swallow from it. He hadn't changed at all since high school—well, that wasn't really true. He'd matured into his features; if anything, he was better looking today than he had been back then.

He arched one eyebrow at her and she flushed. "The years have been good to you," she said, trying to find the words to ask him to forgive the immature girl she'd been.

"I can't complain," he said. "I've been working hard building my company, but I play hard too."

"You mentioned that you are here for business."

"That's right. I'm doing consulting work for the expansion of the buildings here on the grounds."

Macy tipped her head to the side and studied him. "Who asked you to do that?"

"Brad Price. We went to college together."

"You went to UT Austin?"

"Yes, ma'am."

"I thought you were going to get the hell out of Texas," she said.

"Plans changed. I graduated at the top of our class… so it was cheaper for me to go to a Texas state university."

"I forgot about that. Beauty and brains," she said.

"Ah, no, you were always the beauty," he said.

She tucked a strand of hair behind her ear. That other girl she'd been was as foreign to her now as the thought of living anywhere other than Royal. "I was a little intolerable back then."

"Not at all. You were pretty and confident. Every boy in school wanted you."

"Not anymore," she said. "And there was only one boy I wanted."

"You had me, if that's what you meant. Why aren't you confident now?"

She realized that she was feeling a little bit funky tonight. Almost blue. She wasn't about to say out loud that she was no longer pretty. Not to Chris. Especially when she realized that he might want a little revenge against her for the way she'd treated him back then.

"Just not as shallow as I used to be. After my accident, I started working with the kids in the hospital's Burn Unit and I came to realize that true beauty has nothing to do with physical appearance."

"What has it got to do with?" he asked, taking another long swallow of his beer.

"I can't define it, but I do know that it comes from deep inside. I think it's how a person deals with others," she said.

He shook his head. "You sure have changed."

His name was called for dinner before she could respond. She slid out of the booth and Chris put his hand on the small of her back as they walked toward the dining room. His hand was big and warm through the fabric of her sundress and she was very glad that she'd run into him today. Being with Chris tonight made her realize just how much she'd been missing.

Chris spent the evening realizing why he'd fallen for Macy in the first place. She was funny and lively and had the kind of dry wit that made him laugh. She was also very intelligent and just a little bit shy. The shyness was new. She used to be a different girl.

He guessed that was what the difference really was. Macy was a woman now and life had handed her more than a few surprises. He was almost afraid to trust the woman she was tonight. He'd been burned by her once before.

"Why are you staring at me like that?" she asked, taking a sip of her wine.

"You aren't what I expected you to be," he said, opting for the truth, as he usually did. When he'd first gotten into the development business he had run into vendors who'd say anything to make their company sound good. And Chris had set Richardson Development apart from them by always being up front and never promising what he couldn't deliver. He did the same thing in his personal life.

"In what way?" she asked, leaning forward as if his answer was something she wanted to hear.

"Well, to be honest, when you dumped me I had sort of hoped the years would be unkind to you and that you'd get fat and sort of dumpy."

"Are you disappointed I'm not?" she asked with a laugh. She had an effervescent laugh that made him smile. Just the sound of it was joy. Though to his ears it sounded a bit rusty. As if she hadn't had much to laugh about in recent years, which he knew she hadn't.

He shook his head. How could he wish for her to be anything but the beautiful, sexy woman he saw in front of him? Even in the August heat, she looked cool and untouchable.

"Not at all. But that's not really why I was staring at you. When we were teenagers you seemed like a girl who was going to lead a charmed life, and I was noticing that you don't seem bitter that you haven't."

She shrugged one delicate shoulder and a strand of her honey-blond hair fell forward; she reached up and tucked it back behind her ear. "I can't change what happened, so there is no use lamenting it, right?"

"Not everyone would see it that way." He realized she didn't see anything special in the way she was, but he did. Nothing she said would convince him that she wasn't heroic. He liked the way she seemed to have adjusted to the changes in her life and he was very glad he was the first man to take her out after her surgeries were complete.

"It's just the way I am now. Plus, if not for the accident I wouldn't have started working in the Burn Unit at the hospital."

"You mentioned that before. Are you in the medical profession now?" he asked.

"No. But I'm the administrator of the Reynolds Trust."

"What is that?" Chris asked.

"It's a charitable organization that my father established after my mother died. They give money to different organizations, some relating to medical research and providing care for the uninsured. I took over after college. After I started volunteering in the children's Burn Unit, I added it to one of our charities at the trust. I am also a financial analyst and work at my dad's company."

"You sound very busy. Do you enjoy your work?" he asked.

"I do. What about you? What is it like being a big real estate developer?"

"I do a fair amount of work around the state."

"More than a fair amount. Every time I open the business page there's a new project with your company's name on it."

"Do you think about me whenever you see them?" he asked.

"Maybe."

"Never thought I'd make good, did you?" he asked. He'd spent more than a few late nights over the years thinking about Macy and wondering what she'd make of his success.

"I was young, Chris. I really didn't think much about you and me, or the future."

"We were both young."

"I wasn't sure enough to stand on my own…despite how confident I may have seemed at school," she confessed.

He took a deep swallow of his beer, not wanting to comment on it. No matter his age, he'd fallen hard for Macy. "And now?"

"I don't know, Chris. I'm just starting to figure out who I am. The accident made me reevaluate my life."

"I can see that," he said. "And now you're one of the rabble-rousers trying to get the club to admit women to its roster."

"Yes, I am. I think it's time we shake things up in this part of Texas."

Chris laughed at the way she said it. His business was headquartered in Dallas, which wasn't at all like this part of Texas. Here, attitudes were slower to change and men were still men.

"It will be interesting to see what happens," Chris said. He had a hard time imagining women as full-fledged members of the Texas Cattleman's Club. The traditions of the club were part of what made it so exclusive.

"I think we will win. Women have always had a certain advantage when it comes to negotiating with men," Macy said with a tip of her head and a wink.

Macy had always known how to get her way. Which was probably how he'd ended up dating her to begin with. But now he was older and wiser. He should know better, but he was still turned on by this woman. It wouldn't take much manipulating on her part to make him want to please her.

"True enough. And the women in Royal know how to use it to their advantage." He had experienced her powers of persuasion when they'd been in high school. He'd never been able to deny her a thing. Even when she broke up with him he hadn't been sure it wasn't his fault.

"You say that like it's a bad thing," she said.

"It's not," he said. Since the beginning of time women had figured out how to get men to do what they wanted and that was the beauty of the opposite sexes. "I always liked seeing you smile, so if I have to do something to make that happen again then I guess I'd do it," he said. Even walking away from her, he'd done that to make her happy because her father had been making their lives hell back then.

"What about now? Still like my smile?" she asked. "My teeth have been professionally whitened and straightened and Daddy has always said I could charm the whiskers off a cat with this smile."

He leaned in closer and put his hand under her chin, tipping her head to the left then the right, studying her very pretty mouth. "Can you frown for me?"

She chuckled but then pouted for him. He rubbed his thumb over her lower lip. "Now smile."

She did and it was like taking a punch to the gut. He'd forgotten how powerful his reaction was to a true smile from Macy. And this was a true smile.

"Yes. I think it's safe to say you still have some power over me with that smile." Even after all this time. No other woman that he had met had affected him the way she had. He didn't want to admit it, but he'd thought of her often over the years, and being here with her tonight was very fulfilling.

"I'll have to remember that. How long are you in town, Chris?"

"At least the rest of August. I have a project that I have to oversee in Dallas that I will need to return to for September. Why, anxious to see me leave?" he asked.

"Not at all." She leaned forward and rubbed her index finger over his knuckles. Then she looked up at him, her green gaze meeting his, and he felt everyone else in the dining room disappear. There was just the two of them.

"I would miss you if you left today," she said. "I'm sorry we didn't keep in touch when you left Royal. I think I missed out on seeing the best of you as you matured into the man you are today."

"Me too," he said. "I would have liked to see you before your accident so I would be able to tell you how much more beautiful you are now."

He lifted her hand to his mouth and brushed his lips across the back of it. That little display of affection was really all that this conservative community would allow, but he wanted so much more from Macy, and this time he wasn't going to leave without taking what he wanted.

"I've got a bone to pick with you, Richardson." A booming voice jarred him back to the present. He looked up just in time to see Harrison Reynolds barreling down on their table like a Texas longhorn on a rampage.

He was a tall man with a big stocky build and he wore his success well with his nine-hundred-dollar boots and a Stetson on his head. If anyone looked as if he belonged in the club, it was Harrison.

Reluctantly, Chris let go of Macy's hand. It seemed more than one thing hadn't changed since he'd left Royal all those years ago. He wondered if he'd ever have enough money or be influential enough for Harrison to accept him. Because it was very clear to him that no matter what he'd done so far, Harrison Reynolds still didn't believe Chris was good enough for Macy.

Macy glared at her father. Couldn't she have one night that wasn't marred by…what? Her father didn't know that this was a date. He probably thought she and Chris were here discussing club business.

"What about, Harrison?" Chris said, turning that affable grin on her father.

She hadn't realized that his smile was just part of an act and now she did. Was he playing her to maybe get back a little of his own after the way she'd dumped him? That hardly seemed likely since high school was eons ago, and Chris didn't strike her as the kind of man to hold a grudge.

"Your prejudice against Reynolds Construction. Is there a reason why we aren't good enough to win a place on any of your projects?" Harrison asked. He grabbed a chair from a neighboring table and sat down with them.

"Hello, Macy."

"Hello, Dad," she said.

"I'm sure you must have been high when you bid with us. I don't give anyone preferential treatment," Chris said.

"Bull. You and I have had past dealings, thanks to Macy here."

"Harrison, I would never let anything stand in the way of making money. You should know that better than anyone. I'm sure your bids were too high. Stop by my office tomorrow and I'll run through the records and see what we can find."

Harrison nodded. "I'll be there. I hear you are in the

running to rebuild the headquarters and other parts of the club. I'd like a piece of that."

"Dad," Macy said, sounding extremely exasperated. It was clear she didn't want to be sitting here with him while her dad tried to talk about business.

"*Macy.* Leave this to me and Christopher," he said.

She rolled her eyes and once again tucked a strand of hair behind her ear. "I'll be happy to, but you are intruding on my date. My first date in nearly three years, so I'd appreciate it if you'd move on."

Her dad turned to her and she realized what she'd said. "Wait a minute. Did you say date?"

"Yes, I did," Macy said a little defiantly.

"With Richardson?"

"He is the biggest developer in Texas, Daddy," she said.

And just like that, Chris knew that, as the son of a working class man, if he hadn't made something of himself, he wouldn't be sitting here with Miss Macy Reynolds.

He shook his head. "I'm not sure how I feel about this."

"Dad, don't even think about saying anything else. This isn't up for debate," Macy said.

"Fine. We'll discuss this tomorrow, Richardson."

Her dad stood up and walked away as quickly as he'd joined them, and Macy could only watch him leave, incredulous that he'd managed to talk about business and threaten Chris in one breath. She never quite got used to her father and his larger-than-life business persona.

"Um…sorry?"

Chris laughed. "I don't think anyone can apologize

for that man. It was nothing. If my company is showing a bias against him then I need to know about it."

"Okay. But what about us? I don't want…"

"Things to be like they were before?" he asked. He didn't have to be on *CSI* to figure out what she wanted. He wanted the same thing. A chance to date her and get to know her without her father and all of Royal looking on.

"Yes. I mean, I know they aren't, but I wanted to make sure you knew. I'm sorry for the way I broke up with you," she said, biting her lower lip as she waited for him to respond.

He nodded. "I am too."

He smiled at her. He really liked this woman and her honesty. She was refreshing compared to the women he'd been dating lately who were always trying to be what he wanted them to be instead of just being themselves. Macy wasn't like that.

"Not a problem. So, where were we? I believe you mentioned that you'd miss me if I weren't here," he said.

"Did I? I can't remember. Why would I miss you?" she asked.

"Because we didn't have a chance to really get to know each other when we were kids," Chris explained. She'd always been the one girl he'd never been able to forget. He hadn't spent the years pining over her or anything like that, but Macy would just pop up in his thoughts from time to time. Like in fall when the bluebells would blanket the fields near his office, he'd always remember the first time he kissed her and how sweet and innocent that kiss had been.

"You might be right. You were really into football back then," she said. "I remember because that is how I first noticed you. Catching all those passes and making touchdowns. You gave me something to cheer about."

"I remember you cheering me on to many touchdowns."

"I sure did. My squad was the best… That sure was a long time ago. I thought the sun rose and fell on Royal and that the rest of the world was missing out on something," she said.

"Did you ever leave?" he asked, and realized aside from the accident he didn't really know much more about the "new" Macy.

"No. I like it here. I guess I'm just a small-town Texas girl at heart. I probably seem a little unsophisticated for the likes of you now that you're a city slicker."

"No one would ever call you unsophisticated," Chris said. He thought that Macy hadn't left Royal because she hadn't needed to. She had always been part of the upper crust and she'd had more opportunities than he'd had.

"Well, I do read all the fashion magazines," she said with a slight flush.

"And shop at the big stores?" he asked.

"Not recently. I…I really haven't left the house much," she said, putting a hand up when he would have interrupted. "I'm not saying that to make you feel sorry for me. I just read *Vogue* and *Cosmo* and *InStyle* and dreamed of a time when I'd look in the mirror again."

He reached over and took her hand. Holding it in his bigger one. He stroked his thumb over her knuckles as a wave of strong emotion washed over him. Macy wasn't putting up any barriers between them. He was getting the real woman and that made him want to protect her. To make sure that the vulnerable woman who was slowly rediscovering herself had the chance to grow. And he knew he would have to tread carefully with Harrison because he didn't want Macy's father to be an obstacle between Macy and him as he had been in the past.

"Surely you don't have those doubts after today," Chris said.

"I...I wish it were that easy, Chris, but to be honest, a part of me is still afraid of seeing the scars when I look in the mirror. Not sure I believe the reflection I saw was real."

He reached up and stroked her cheek, though he knew better than to let this go too far in public. There was something fragile...almost broken...about Macy and he couldn't let it go. No matter that she'd broken his heart in the past, he saw that she was a different woman now. "Let me tell you what I see."

She nodded and held her breath, her pretty white teeth biting her lower lip as he stared at her face. And he wondered how bad her scars had been before the plastic surgery. He'd never met anyone who'd been in a life-threatening accident before.

He traced the high line of her cheekbone over her smooth alabaster skin. Her eyebrows were dark blond. "I see skin like the palest marble, so pretty and smooth."

He moved his finger over her lips. They were full and plump, utterly kissable, and he longed to taste her again. "I see a mouth so pink and delectable it's all I can do to resist kissing you."

He rubbed his finger over the line of her jaw. "This strong jaw tells me that you still haven't lost the stubbornness that's always been a part of you."

She gave him a little half smile. He ran his finger

over the arch of her eyebrows—first one then the other. "These pretty green eyes watch me with a combination of weariness and curiosity. I don't want to disappoint you."

She captured his hand and held it to her cheek. "Thank you, Chris."

He knew whatever else happened between the two of them that he wasn't leaving Royal until Macy was the beautiful flirt she used to be. Confident of herself and her ability to attract every man in the area—especially him.

Three

Macy left Chris after dinner to powder her nose. He was a little intense and she wasn't as ready for him as she might have been, say, four years earlier. Chris had changed in his time away from Royal and her. And she hoped she'd changed as well, but she had the feeling that her changes hadn't taken her as far forward as Chris's had taken him.

"Macy?"

She glanced up in the mirror and saw Abby standing in the doorway. Her friend looked fabulous as always and Macy knew she should stop comparing herself to every woman in the room at some point, but she had no idea when and if that would happen.

"Hello, there. What are you doing here?" she asked Abby.

"Promoting myself to become the next president. I can't let any time slip by. How's dinner?" Abby asked.

She shook her long red wavy hair. Her blue eyes had always made Macy envious. She'd always wanted pretty eyes like that instead of the green ones she had. But after her surgeries she was very happy with her eyes now.

Macy blushed and then shook her head. "Nice. Dad stopped by and read Chris the riot act for not using his company, but Chris calmly stood his ground. I've never seen anyone handle Daddy like that."

Abby laughed and slung her arm around Macy's shoulders. "It's about time. You okay?"

"Yes," Macy said, then realized that she was telling the truth. She hadn't felt like this in a long time. She wanted to laugh for no good reason and just shout at the top of her lungs that life was good. "I really am."

"Good," Abby said.

Macy left the ladies' room and went back to their table. She saw that Chris was talking to a tall handsome African-American man that Macy didn't know. She wasn't sure if she should approach the table because they seemed engrossed in whatever they were discussing, but Chris glanced up and waved her over.

"Zeke, this is Macy Reynolds, Harrison's daughter, Macy this is Zeke Travers. He and I went to college together."

Zeke Travers was solid and muscular with a shaved head and dark brown skin. He had kind eyes and smiled when he glanced over at her.

"It's a pleasure to meet you," Macy said, holding out her hand.

"You as well," Zeke said. "I'll let you get back to dinner. Drinks tomorrow?"

"You're on," Chris said.

Zeke left and Macy watched him go. Brad Price walked straight up to Zeke, and Macy could tell he wasn't happy. The sounds of raised voices could be heard throughout the room and everyone watched them.

"What is going on with them?" Macy asked. She couldn't help herself—she was naturally curious about the spectacle the men were making. Brad pulled a piece of paper from his pocket and waved it at Zeke.

"I have no idea," Chris said. "I'll try to find out more from Zeke tomorrow when we have drinks."

"I sound like a small-town gossip, don't I?" she asked. She wished she wasn't nosy, but she always had been. She liked knowing what was going on in other people's lives.

"It's the nature of Royal to talk," Chris said. Brad looked beet-red with fury. Whatever was upsetting him it had to be serious. She'd never seen Brad in such a state before.

"I hope he's okay," Macy said. She and Brad weren't close friends or anything, but she knew him from Texas Cattleman's Club events when they were children.

"Who is?" Abby said, coming up to their table.

"Brad," Chris said, gesturing to the two men who were arguing.

"He's probably just learned that I am making serious inroads to becoming the next president of the club," Abby said with a confident grin.

"Are you?" Chris asked, arching one eyebrow at her and giving her a hard stare.

"Indeed I am. And you are...?" Abby asked.

"Forgive my manners," Macy said. "Abigail Langley, this is Christopher Richardson. Abby is going to be the next president of the club. Chris has been asked to come up with a development plan for the new headquarters building. He owns his own development company out of Dallas."

Abby and Chris had run in different circles in high school. Well, to be honest, Abby and Macy had run in different circles. Macy's life had been cheerleading and parties at TCC and Chris had fallen in with her crowd by being a football star. Abby and she hadn't had much in common then.

The two shook hands and Abby took a seat in the chair recently vacated by Zeke. Of the three people they'd had at the table she was happiest to have her good friend there now. She wanted Abby's opinion on Chris. It wasn't that she didn't trust her instincts when it came to men—wait a minute, it was exactly that she didn't trust them.

She'd been engaged to a man who'd left her the minute she wasn't the Texas beauty she'd always been. She didn't want to chance getting hurt again.

And though this was only a dinner date, it was with Chris Richardson. The boy she'd defied her father to date. He'd always been attractive to her. Not just physically, though there was that.

"Macy?" Abby asked, startling Macy out of her thoughts.

"Yes?"

"I asked if you thought that Chris and I would work well together when I'm president," Abby said.

She had to give it to Abby for being persistent and determined. There wasn't a person in Royal who didn't know what Abby's intent was. She was focused one hundred percent on becoming the first female president of the Texas Cattleman's Club. "Yes, I do."

Abby smiled at her friend and then reached over to squeeze her hand before getting up. "I'll leave you to your dinner. It was nice meeting you, Chris."

"You too," Chris said.

Abby left and Macy sat back in her chair. "I'd forgotten what it's like to come to dinner at the club. It's such a hub for everyone."

"You really haven't been out for a while?" Chris asked. He took a sip of his drink and leaned forward when he talked to her. It was a very intimate thing to do and made her feel as if they were the only two people here tonight.

"For years." At first she'd been horrified and so traumatized by everything that had happened that she'd been afraid to leave the house. Then she'd wanted to go out, but the few forays she'd made had shown her that people stared. She hadn't been strong enough for that.

"Well, how do you think it went then?" Chris asked. "Your first dinner out in years."

"I think it went well," Macy admitted. "It's also my first date in years."

She'd been hiding away at her father's ranch trying to pretend that she'd just moved from her hometown. It had been hard being so badly injured in a place where she'd known so many people. She had needed to just blend in and that wasn't possible in Royal, so she'd started staying home.

"I'm glad," Chris admitted. "I'm not happy about the circumstances that led to it, but I'm very honored to be the first man you've been out with."

She didn't want to let this mean too much. Chris wasn't in town looking for a small-town girl as his wife, and she knew she was vulnerable right now. But she had enjoyed herself and their date and, if she was honest, she'd have to say she hoped he'd ask her out again.

"I'm glad it was you too," she said. "You have made my night, and celebrating my first day free of bandages couldn't have been nicer. Thank you, Chris."

"It was truly my pleasure, Macy."

The feeling of being in a fishbowl when he went out in Royal was very different from what he usually felt in Dallas. In the big city, no one noticed who he was with, but tonight he was very aware that most of the town knew he and Macy had had dinner together. The gossip had defined who he was and had served to make him want to be better than his dad. He'd been only too happy to shake the dust of this town from his feet.

"I'd kind of forgotten what Royal was like."

"I bet. Don't miss it much, do you?" she asked as he paid the bill and they sat for an extra minute to talk and drink the Baileys that Chris had ordered for them.

"I miss my mom," he admitted. "She's Royal born and bred. I've tried to get her to move up to Dallas but she won't do it, keeps trying to make me move back here instead."

"What about your dad?" Macy asked.

"Nah, he was a Yankee," Chris said with a laugh. "East Coaster who fell in love with the oil industry thanks to the movie *Giant*. Mom used to tease him that he came to Royal looking for Liz Taylor."

"Your mom is pretty enough. Did he think he'd found her?" Macy asked.

"Yes, I think he did. They had a happy marriage until he passed."

"I was sorry to hear about your loss," Macy said. "Did you get the flowers I sent?"

"I don't know. Mom handled all that," he said. That entire time was still a blur for him. He hadn't been old enough to have made his peace with his dad. He had been getting closer to forgiving the old man for all the things he hadn't done for him. Things that a boy had wanted but a man knew weren't really important. "Why didn't you come to the funeral?"

His dad had died when Chris had been a junior in college. It had changed his perspective and sharpened his desires to make his life different. He'd stopped being such a frat boy and focused more on his studies.

"I didn't think I'd be welcome," Macy said. "But I remembered meeting him and how sweet he'd been to me. He was a nice man. Your parents were always so funny at dinner, teasing you and treating you like...the apple of their eye."

"Only when we had company. They had plenty of fault to find when we were alone."

Unlike her dad, who'd forbidden Macy to see Chris, his parents had adored her and really treated her well when she'd come to dinner at his house. But Chris and his dad had butted heads a lot, something his mom had said was due to the fact that they were both stubborn as mules. Chris suspected it was more likely that they both wanted different things for him.

"Ready to go?" he asked, changing the subject.

"I guess so. I've really enjoyed tonight, Chris," she said. In fact, she couldn't remember a date she'd enjoyed more in her adult life. Benjamin had been a coworker of hers and they'd kind of fallen into dating because all their friends were coupled up. They had found each other by default, she thought. Maybe that was why they hadn't lasted.

"Me too," he said, his voice a rich deep baritone that brushed over her senses like a cool breeze on a hot summer's day.

He put his hand on the small of her back as he directed her through the dining room toward the outer doors of the club. He liked the feel of her under his hands. They'd been too young when they'd dated before to get into anything other than heavy petting. And he remembered her teenage body in a bikini from the summer, but that was all. He wondered what she looked like now.

She stopped and started laughing as she saw the sea of pink flamingos.

"What's so funny?" Chris asked.

"The flamingos. I can't believe they showed up here," Macy said. No one was supposed to know who exactly had placed the birds, so she had to pretend she didn't know. The lawn of the club was dotted with gaudy pink flamingos and Chris had a chuckle as well.

"I guess it was the club's time," Chris said. "Mother said one of her neighbors had them a few weeks ago."

"It definitely is the club's time to have them here. I think they're cute," she said.

The conversation trailed off and he could do nothing but stare at her in the moonlight. He took her hand and led her down one of the many paths and out of sight of prying eyes. Her thick honey-blond hair hung loosely around her shoulders.

"Why do you keep looking at me?" she asked.

"I've never seen anyone quite as beautiful," he said.

It was the truth, and all that he knew about her had just been enhanced tonight.

"That's not true, but I'm going to say thank-you anyway."

"It is true," he said. Years ago her question would have been blatant flirting, but today he sensed her genuine unease about her own looks. "How can I convince you of what I see when I look at you?"

She shrugged and nibbled on her lower lip, which drew his eyes to her mouth. He loved her mouth, even with the tiny scar on her upper lip. The full lower lip that made him just want to lean down and taste her. He wanted her.

No big shock there. She was stunningly beautiful, even though she seemed to have forgotten that. He was here for business in the place that he used to call home but where he'd felt he never fit in. And now he didn't want to think about business or fitting in. Macy dominated every thought.

"I don't know. I think I've been afraid to take chances," she said.

"Is dinner with me a chance?" he asked.

She gave him a wistful half smile. "I think it is."

He took her hand in his and led her away from the club toward the flock of pink flamingos. Stopping right in front of them, he pulled her into his arms and tipped her chin up.

"I've been wanting to do this since we ran into each other at the hospital."

"Hold me?" she asked, licking her lips.

"No, I'll kiss you instead," he said. He lowered his head and gave her a chaste kiss. The kind that would have been acceptable when they'd been dating in high school. But her mouth opened on a sigh and her warm breath stole into his. And he groaned because he wanted more.

What he felt for Macy went way beyond the chaste and pure. He angled his mouth over hers and made teasing forays with his tongue. Tasting the essence of this fragile, pretty woman with each sweep of his tongue.

She moaned softly and her hands clung to his shoulders as he slid his hands down her back to her waist and drew her closer to him. He hadn't felt anything this strong…well, in a while. Lust was something he'd dealt with before, but with Macy it was stronger than it ever had been.

He wanted more than to sweep her off her feet and into his bed. That should have been warning, but the only bells going off in his head were screaming for him to remove her clothing and touch her flesh. He wanted her.

He pulled back, but her eyes were closed and her mouth dewy and soft. He couldn't resist coming back for another kiss. Her taste was addictive and the feel of her in his arms even more unforgettable than he'd believed it could be.

"Chris…"

"Yes?"

"I liked that. I can't think of a better gift to celebrate my last surgery than this night and you," she told him once more.

He hugged her close and she rested her head on his shoulder. He stroked his hand down her back. This moment was almost perfect. He was on the lawn of the club that had eluded him as a young man. A place he'd stood looking in on many times, but where he was now welcome.

He held the woman that he hadn't been good enough for all those years ago and she wasn't asking him to sneak around with her, but instead stood here in full view of anyone choosing to glance at them.

And she'd called him a gift. She had no idea how often he'd dreamed of this moment as a teenager or how different it actually was than what he'd fantasized about it. Macy made the difference. Perhaps he still wanted revenge on her dad, but the feeling wasn't as sharp as it once had been.

When Macy had first woken up in the hospital three years ago she hadn't wanted to live. She couldn't accurately describe the pain to anyone who'd never been severely burned, but she'd wanted to die from it. She'd spent each day in an agony of tears and melancholy. Then Dr. Webb had suggested she leave her room and go down to the children's Burn Unit.

One visit was all it had taken for her to stop feeling so overwhelmed. She was amazed at how the kids, some of whom were burned far more badly that she was, just sort of soldiered on. She'd started visiting them at least once a week ever since.

Macy walked into the hospital burn ward the way she always did—feeling as if she was coming home. She had a real job—financial analyst for Reynolds Construction—but this was where she really belonged.

She went immediately to the play area where children scarred by burns and recovering from their own surgeries spent time playing without having anyone stare at them. Sara, a twelve-year-old who'd been trapped in a house fire and had burns on her entire left side, was the first one to notice Macy. The little girl's hair would never grow back, and despite the many surgeries she'd endured, she'd been slow to recover. But Macy had been in worse shape than Sara when she'd come to the hospital.

"You're beautiful," Sara said, a big smile growing across her face. "I know you said you used to be pretty, but you are way better than pretty, Miss Macy."

"Thank you. I wasn't sure what to expect when the bandages came off. I was so scared I almost couldn't look at myself in the mirror."

"Dr. Webb told me that if you recovered I could," Sara said.

She knew that Sara had been anxious for her to complete her surgery so she'd know what it would be like for herself. Who could fault the twelve-year-old for wanting an adult to go through it first? Dr. Webb had suggested Macy start spending time here during her treatment. All the surgeries and the long recovery periods had taken a toll on Macy and she'd felt so isolated, like many of the kids here.

"That's good news. I bet you are going to be even more beautiful than I am when he's done, because you already are," Macy said, rubbing her hand over Sara's head.

Sara smiled at her and gave her a hug. She was in the hospital this time for another surgery on her arms, which had damage as well.

"I brought you a few fashion magazines."

"Yes! I have a new friend here—Jen. She came in yesterday. She's very sad, Macy."

"I'm sorry to hear that. What do you think will cheer her up?" Macy asked.

"Maybe a makeover like we did," Sara said.

Macy nodded. Almost a year ago, when she was feeling at her lowest, she'd had a moment of inspiration. Or maybe it had just been pure stubbornness. Instead of feeling so ugly, she'd decided to hell with it and sponsored an afternoon of fun for the girls in the ward. She'd brought in a local spa company and then gave all the girls pedicures. Just pretty bright nails that they could glance down at and see whenever they felt as if the surgeries were never going to stop and the burns were never going to go away.

"It will take me a few days to arrange it. When does she go home?"

"Not for three weeks. I'm here that long too," Sara said.

"Okay, I will do it."

"Thanks, Macy. I'm ready to look at those magazines now," Sara said.

Macy handed the stack she'd brought to the little girl and then sat next to her on the couch, flipping through the pages. They talked about clothes, and that gave her the idea to maybe have a little fashion show on the ward too. She could bring in some real clothes for the girls to try on. Anything would be better than the hospital gowns the kids were forced to wear.

Then she remembered that Chris's mom was a seamstress and decided to ask her to help design some new gowns for the children. The gowns would have to be lightweight and flowing to accommodate bandages and such. Macy began to feel excited about her idea.

She hoped his mother would feel up to working on the project.

She left the burn ward almost an hour later and stepped out into the August heat. The temperature was in the triple digits and even the linen sundress she wore felt too heavy.

"Macy." Chris called her name just as she got to her car. It was such a hot day that she remote-started it and hit a button to make sure the air conditioner was running before she got in. Summer was one of her favorite seasons, but this August was too hot and she barely tolerated it.

"What are you doing here?" she asked as she turned to face him. He wore a pair of dress pants and a shirt and tie. His thick blond hair hung loosely around the back of his neck and his aviator-style sunglasses blocked his eyes from view.

"Picking my mom up. She's being discharged today," he said. She could tell from the way he said it that he was happy to see his mother recovering, and who could blame him. Macy knew from experience that being in the hospital wasn't fun. And having to visit someone who was ill was even harder.

"That's great news," Macy said. She glanced at her watch and realized she could probably squeeze another hour of time out of her day to go with Chris and help with his mom. "Do you want some company?" She hit the button to turn off her car.

Chris tipped his head. "Your dad and I had a contentious discussion this morning—does that matter to you?"

"Was it about me?" she asked. She really hoped not. Her dad should be able to keep his distance from her personal life. And if he couldn't then she'd have to have a little talk with him. Despite the fact that she'd needed him the past few years, she didn't want him interfering in her budding relationship with Chris.

"No. We were talking about business. He wanted to make sure I didn't forget I'd said I would try to look into the bids he submitted to us," Chris said.

"Then I don't care. I run my little spreadsheets and give Dad the numbers he needs... Oh, no, I hope none of my figures cost him a bid."

"I'm sure you didn't. And I think it's a good idea for you to keep your distance. Your dad is a bull when it comes to that construction company," Chris said. "I'd stay out of it myself if I could. I should have realized coming back to Royal wasn't going to be easy,"

"Yes, you should have. Plus, working on the club is highly controversial—everyone has their own ideas about what it is and how it should be," Macy said. "Ask Abby. She is trying so hard to make some changes at the Texas Cattleman's Club, but it isn't as easy as she thought it would be."

"At least I'm just here to bid on a job. I don't know if I could put up with some of the older guard if I was Abby," Chris said.

"She has a way of handling things," Macy said. If there was one thing her redheaded friend had it was determination, and she'd keep on something like the club letting in women until the men simply gave in.

"Dogged stubbornness?" Chris asked.

Macy laughed. That did seem to sum up Abby. "She's not going to back down."

"Reminds me of another woman I know."

"Who do you mean?"

"You," he said. He linked their hands together and drew her back toward the hospital. "You have never given up on yourself when others would have."

"You mean because of the surgeries?" she asked.

"Yes, and the fact that you aren't bitter about anything that's happened to you. You have no idea how remarkable that is," he said.

She was touched that he thought so. There had been times when she'd wanted to lock herself in her room and never leave it again. But she'd always had a reason to leave. Especially once Dr. Webb asked her to visit the kids in the Burn Unit. They gave her so much courage. But she didn't mention that. Didn't want to share something so private with Chris. Not yet. They were still trying to figure out who they were now.

Macy followed Chris into his mother's room. She sat on the edge of her bed wearing a pair of jeans and a sleeveless top. "It's about time you got here."

"Sorry, Mom. I ran into some trouble at the office and then Macy. She's going to keep you company while I go see about your discharge papers." Chris gave his mother a kiss on the cheek and then left the room.

"You look well," Margaret said a little coolly.

"Thank you. I feel good," Macy said. "How about you?"

"Much better. My doctor just worries about my heart, but it's fine."

"Are you sure?" Macy asked, knowing that Chris would be devastated if anything happened to his mom.

"Yes, I am," Margaret said.

It was clear that Margaret hadn't really forgiven Macy for dumping Chris the way she had. And Macy was just now realizing the full extent of her actions back then. The old Macy would have given up, but now she was determined to try to rebuild the trust that Margaret used to have in her.

"I could use your help. I seem to remember you liked to sew."

"I still do," she said defensively. "I don't see what that has to do with you."

She wasn't making this easy on Macy. "Well, I have some friends in the children's Burn Unit and I need someone who can sew who can help me out. Are you interested?"

"Maybe. Tell me more about what you have in mind," she said.

"I want to have a makeover day for the kids in the Burn Unit and I thought we could replicate for them some of the fashions they see in magazines. I can't buy the clothes off the shelves because some of the kids have serious skin-sensitivity issues. If you're interested, I'm going to talk to Dr. Webb and the other specialists and see what they need," Macy said.

"I'd love to help out," Margaret said. "I need a project at home."

"Good," Macy said.

Chris came back a few minutes later with an orderly and a wheelchair and they left the hospital. He kept watching her and she felt a little giddy from the attention. When he asked her if she was available for dinner she said yes.

Four

"Do you think you can do it?" Brad Price asked.

Chris was sitting in the clubhouse throwing back a pint with Brad as they discussed the pros and cons and costs of building a new Texas Cattleman's Club headquarters.

The years had been good to Brad, who'd always been athletic. He was well-groomed and very preppy in his look. Even a stranger would be able to tell he'd been born with a silver spoon in his mouth. His family had long been members of the Texas Cattleman's Club.

"Of course I can," Chris said. "My office is working on the project as we speak and I will have the report to you as soon as it's completed. I think that the new headquarters will be a good direction for the club."

"I do too," Brad said. "I want our generation to make a mark on the club. When I go into the dining room I feel like I'm sixteen and sneaking in without my dad's permission. It should feel like it belongs to us."

"Should I be concerned about the upcoming election?" Chris asked. He didn't want to spend a ton of man-hours working on the project only to have it all be for nothing if Brad didn't win the presidency.

"Why would you?" Brad asked.

"Just in case you aren't elected…"

"That's blasphemy." Brad shook his head. "This is Royal, Texas, not some big city like Dallas. Our members aren't about to vote for a woman president. She's only a member because of how much we all loved Richard."

Chris rubbed the back of his neck. "Damn shock."

"No kidding. We all depended on him here. It's different for you, Chris, because you're new blood as far as the club is concerned but for all of us old-timers who grew up with a Langley in the club—we didn't know what to do. The old guard was feeling sentimental…"

"So they extended an invite to Abby with full privileges never suspecting she was going to stir things up and try to become president."

"Exactly," Brad said, taking a long draw on his beer. "Women!"

Chris lifted his glass in a mock toast and then took a swallow of his beer. Actually, Chris had to admit that he had no problem with any of the changes that the women wanted made at the Texas Cattleman's Club. He thought that it was about time that women had rights at the club. As Brad had said earlier, it wasn't their dads' generation anymore—it was theirs.

"So is everything good with you?" Chris asked, thinking of the fight he'd seen between Zeke and Brad last night. He knew that to Brad, the question might appear to have come out of the blue, but Chris wasn't much on subtlety.

Brad gave him a hard stare and looked distinctly uncomfortable. "Yes. Why do you ask?"

"I saw you and Zeke arguing last night when I was in here having dinner. You're normally not quick-tempered…" Chris let the sentence fall off. He didn't want to push, but he and Brad had been friends in college and, if the other man had troubles, Chris would help him out.

"It was nothing. Just a minor disagreement over something not related to the club," Brad said, looking more than a little distracted. "I noticed you were dining with a woman."

"It was Macy Reynolds."

"I hadn't realized she had fully recovered. That was a really bad accident. Her dad was broken up when it first happened. Spent a lot of nights at the club drinking," Brad said. "She looks good now."

"Well, the bandages from her last surgery came off yesterday. We were having dinner to celebrate," Chris said, not sure he liked the fact that Brad had noticed her looks. "She does look good."

"That's great news. I haven't kept in touch with her, but I guess you did," Brad said.

No one really knew that Macy's dad had forced Chris out of her life. That wasn't the kind of thing that he'd wanted to talk about at UT Austin, so he'd just said they'd drifted apart back then. Who wanted to tell people that he wasn't good enough for the girl he loved? Maybe a different man than he was, but Chris had kept his mouth shut back then.

"No, we didn't. I ran into her at the hospital," Chris said.

Brad nodded at him. "Visiting your mom, right? Is she better?"

"The doctors still don't know what's wrong with her heart. One of them pulled me aside and suggested that since these episodes happen regular as clockwork, perhaps I ought to consider visiting more often."

"Maybe you should."

Chris shrugged. Brad was Royal's golden boy. He himself had been a poor kid. Someone whose parents were around town but weren't part of the in-crowd. He hadn't minded it when he'd been younger. Because when you were in elementary school it didn't matter if you were rich or poor. Everyone played together and got along. Then somewhere around seventh grade everything started changing and groups started forming that had a hard money dividing line.

"I just always wanted more than Royal had to offer," Chris said. And he still did. Though Macy interested him a lot and he could only find her here.

"Do you still want more?" Brad asked. "This little town is changing."

"You just said we aren't like Dallas," Chris pointed out. He liked Dallas. It was more metropolitan than the rest of the state, certainly more so than Royal. There were a lot of people from other parts of the country living in Dallas these days and they'd brought their attitudes with them.

"Well, it would be different for you. Having a woman president of the Texas Cattle*man's* Club isn't going to happen."

"So you say," Chris said. But he knew that all attitudes hadn't changed. The older generation—like Harrison Reynolds—would be only too happy to show Chris the door.

The club looked exactly as it was meant to, a luxury club for the wealthy and privileged in Texas. The heavy furniture was large and comfy for a man, but dwarfed the women when they came to sit in the cozy room. The paneling was dark and on one wall were televisions tuned to industry- and financial-news stations. In another corner, ESPN played. The club wasn't welcoming to women and he didn't see how Abby was going to change that.

As Brad had said, this was Royal. An old Texas oil-rich town with lots of old Texas values. He doubted that anyone who hadn't lived here would get what he meant by that, because Texas was different. Men still held doors open for women and took care of their wives and put God and football first.

Chris shook his head thinking about it.

"Thanks for meeting me today, Chris."

"Not a problem. I'll have some preliminary estimates to you this evening for what it would take to renovate and enhance the existing clubhouse. The new buildings will take me a few days."

"Not a problem."

Brad and he finished their beers and Chris left as one of the other club members drifted over to talk to Brad. It didn't matter that he'd been afforded full privileges as an honorary member, he still felt like an outsider.

He saw Abby standing in the doorway looking in as well. He wondered if she felt the same way. He smiled at her when she looked up and waved as he turned and walked out of the clubhouse.

He toyed with the idea that the situation with Macy

was just like the clubhouse and Abby. She wanted to think the world around her had changed and, since he had money now, her dad wouldn't try to interfere in a relationship between them, but he suspected that old attitudes hadn't changed that much.

His cell phone rang when he got to his car and he glanced at the caller ID before answering it. It was a Royal area code, but he didn't recognize the number.

"This is Richardson."

"Chris? It's Macy."

"Hello, there, what can I do for you?" he asked.

"Um…do you want to meet me for an early-morning horseback ride tomorrow?" she asked.

"At your ranch?"

"No at Tom's Stables. Do you know where it is?"

"I do. Okay, what time?"

"Six," she said.

"That's early but I'll be there," he said.

"Bye."

She hung up before he could say goodbye and he pocketed his phone. He hadn't been on a horse in years but he wasn't about to say no to Macy. It was the one thing he'd wanted her to do back when they were in high school. Take the initiative in their relationship.

Macy woke up at 5:00 a.m. and dressed in her jodhpurs, fitted shirt and riding jacket. She'd pick up her helmet at the stables. Riding had been the one thing that she'd been able to continue doing even when she'd been scarred. She drove through the early-morning streets of Royal. It was warm but not hot on this August morning.

She pulled into the parking lot and saw Chris leaning against the hood of his Porsche. It was a flashy car, and she suspected that was why he'd driven it today. He wore the trappings of his success well, and she regretted she'd let her dad talk her out of dating him so many years before. If they'd stayed together, she probably would have been on a different path, hopefully with him.

"Morning," she said, getting out of her car. She used to drive a cute Audi convertible, but now had a big Cadillac that her father bought for her. It was a heavy car and was one of the top-rated in safety upon impact.

"Morning. I haven't been on a horse in years," Chris said as he walked over to her. "You look like you're ready for a dressage competition."

"I'm not," she said. She'd never been a competitive person by nature, and really it was the routine of riding she liked better than the winning of awards and accolades. "Let me get my crop and helmet out of the trunk."

"Take your time. The stable manager is getting our horses ready. My mom packed us a breakfast picnic." Chris looked so sexy this morning. It didn't help matters that last night all she'd dreamed about was that kiss they'd shared in front of the flamingos. She wanted so much more than just sweet passion-filled kisses from him. But she wasn't sure he was on the same page.

To him she was probably just an old friend that he was spending time with until he left Royal. Maybe not a platonic friend, she thought, remembering the intensity of the kiss they'd shared after dinner. But not a woman he was bent on dating either. She reckoned that had a lot to do with their past and the way she'd treated him.

"That was sweet of her," Macy said as she grabbed her equipment and walked over to Chris.

"She's probably hoping you and I will fall in love and give her some grandbabies."

Macy dropped her crop. *Um...that's a lot more than dating,* she thought. And she'd never imagined he'd even consider that. Now she was hearing... "What? We're barely dating."

Chris laughed. "I told her the same thing. She said a woman can hope, especially a woman who'd just come out of the hospital. I told her she was pushing it. But she just winked and laughed at me."

Macy laughed, as she was sure that Chris intended her to, but inside she was quaking with fear. She had just gotten through a very trying time in her life and she wanted some fun with Chris. She didn't want to think any further than the end of this week.

A big part of her wanted to retreat to her father's house and her bedroom. She wanted to lock herself away and keep herself safe from anything like this. To anyone else, a sexy man saying things about love and babies might be ideal, but not to her. She still wasn't whole and sometimes she felt as if she never would be.

"I'm not—"

"It's okay. I was just being silly. I'm not going to try to talk you into marrying me."

Macy looked at Chris. His tight-fitting jeans and plain black T-shirt so nondescript and yet so defining of the man he was. He might drive a Porsche and run, according to her dad, a billion-dollar development company. But she knew that at heart he was still this man.

If this was six months from now and she'd had time to recover from the past three years of not knowing how she was going to look or when she was going to regain her life, she'd probably do everything in her power to get him to propose. But right now…she just wasn't ready.

"It's not you," she said. "I'm barely able to believe that I have my life back."

"And you're not ready for a commitment. I know. We're just dating and renewing an old friendship," he said.

She tried to read his body language and see if he wanted more than friendship, but it was impossible to tell.

A horse whinnied and they both turned to see Tom, the owner of the stables, walking toward them leading a chestnut horse. "Mr. Richardson, your horse is ready."

"Thank you, Tom."

"Anne will be along with your horse in a minute, Macy," he said to her. "You're looking mighty fine without those bandages on."

"Thank you, Mr. Tom," she said.

"You're welcome, ma'am. Anne's prayer group has been keeping you on the top of their list. I think they will be happy to know that you have recovered."

Macy was touched by his wife's concern. "That means more than I can say."

Tom nodded and then walked away. She hugged herself with one arm, acknowledging that even though she'd felt really alone over the past three years, she hadn't been.

Chris walked over to his horse and took the saddle as if he'd been born in it. She watched as he walked the horse around the yard a few times and then came back to her side just as Anne brought Macy's horse, Buttercup, out.

Macy led the horse to the mounting block, donned her helmet and took her own saddle. She probably didn't need a helmet for this short ride, but her doctors had been adamant when she'd first started riding again that she always don protective gear, and she found she liked doing it now. It was part of her routine and she wasn't going to give it up.

"I'll follow you," Chris said.

Macy glanced over her shoulder at him as she led the way out. Chris followed her down a path through a wooded area behind the stables, and when the path was wide enough he moved his horse up beside her.

"How often do you come out here?" he asked, his deep voice making her want to ask him to just keep on talking.

"Three times a week. It was the only thing I could do for a while. Tom and Anne never stared at my scars or me. And when I was still using a walker, they helped me get onto the horse."

"Wasn't that dangerous?" he asked, concern in his voice.

"What?" she asked. The rides she'd taken while recovering had been the impetus she needed some days not to sink into sadness.

"Riding on your own while you needed a walker?" he asked.

She shook her head. Thinking about how weak she'd been in the beginning. Her damn right thigh with the missing muscle had ached, but once she'd set her mind on riding, she had been determined to see it through. "Tom would follow me about fifty yards or so back."

"Why didn't he just ride with you?" Chris asked.

"I needed to do it on my own," she said, pulling

Buttercup's reins so the horse stopped. Chris stopped riding as well. She remembered those first rides when she'd just cried the entire time. The emotions of being outside and doing something familiar had been more than she could handle at first.

Chris reached over and put his hand on hers. "I'm sorry you had to go through that alone."

"I had to. It was either prove to myself that I could do it or disappear from society completely and just live in Daddy's house the rest of my life."

"But you're not dependent anymore. You're fully healed, so when are you moving out?" Chris asked.

"That's right, I am. I'm going to move back to my own home in a couple of weeks. I don't want you to think I'm weak. The doctors wouldn't let me live on my own when they first released me from the hospital...and Daddy, well, he didn't want to let me out of his sight. I almost died."

Chris leaned over and pulled her toward him. Kissing her hard and passionately. Then he sat back in his own saddle and kicked his horse into a trot. She watched him ride away and then urged Buttercup to follow.

She had the feeling that Chris didn't like hearing about what almost happened to her. None of her friends had, but Chris was the first one who had made her feel as if he would have really missed her if she'd died in the hospital after her accident. As though their journey with each other would have been cut short.

And despite what she'd said earlier, she realized that a part of her did want to have a solid relationship with Chris. She almost felt safe dreaming about a future with him and maybe children of her own. And that was thanks to Chris.

* * *

Chris didn't like thinking about what might have been. He'd left Royal and had shaken the past from his boots like dust as he'd walked away. But if Macy had died three years ago… He didn't like the feeling that thought evoked in him. He was used to being in control and he'd just been presented with the very real proof that he wasn't really in control of anything.

"Chris," Macy called.

He slowed his horse, but seeing her sitting on her own just made him long to pull her into his arms again.

He really needed to get his head together and he didn't want to talk to Macy right now. He felt raw. And the last time he'd felt that way had been when his father had died.

"You okay?" she asked.

He shook his head. "I hate that you might have died and I would never have had the chance to know you again."

She swallowed then edged her horse closer to his. The morning sun shone down on her and she looked so healthy to him that it was hard to believe she'd struggled to get back to this state for the past few years.

"Me too. I feel like you and me have unfinished business," she said.

"We definitely do," he agreed. He wanted to hold her again and do everything he could to keep her safe, which was silly, because there was no threat to her here. "Let's go back to the stables and return the horses. Will you join me for breakfast?"

"After your mom went to all that trouble to make it, I think I'd better."

They returned the horses to the stables and then walked over to their cars. "Should I follow you?"

"Nah, we can take the Porsche. I have a nice spot picked out not too far from here."

"I thought you had a Range Rover," she said.

"I had this one brought out from Dallas. I like the speed of it."

"I'm not much on going fast," she said.

"I won't let anything happen to you," he said. "Do you believe me?"

"Yes. Yes, I do. Okay, I will ride with you. I can't stay long, though. I have to go in to the office this morning."

"Since you know the boss, I don't think he'll fire you if you're not on time," Chris said. Her father was the central man in her life right now and Chris wanted to be that guy instead. He wanted her to depend on him for everything. Dammit, he wanted more from Macy than dating and renewing old ties. He wanted *her*.

That was a given. But he hadn't realized how important it was for her to see him on the same level as her dad. He couldn't believe he was still showing off and trying to impress her. But he knew that was what bringing the Porsche here was all about. There wasn't one other person in Royal who he wanted to see him in this car other than Macy.

"You're right, but I don't like to take advantage... Actually, Dad gives me lots of leeway at the job because I'm still not one hundred percent... Wait a minute, I am. I keep forgetting I've been through my last surgery. Do you know what that means?" she asked, a slow smile spreading across her pretty face.

"No, what?" he asked, playing along with her.

"That I never have to go to the doctor's again and

hear about my options," she said with a smile. "That is such a relief."

"I'm so glad to hear that."

"Me too. I can't believe I didn't think about that until now," she said.

Chris reached over and drew her into his arms. He held her close to him, feeling the soft exhalation of her breath on his neck, and thanked God that she was alive and wholly recovered. He hadn't been there for her during her darkest days, but he was going to make this period of her life the best he could.

She hugged him tight and he held on to her as if his life depended on it. He tried to convey in that embrace all the things he didn't know how to put into words. Like how scary it was to think of her hurt or weighing options.

"So, where are we having breakfast?" she asked.

Reluctantly he let her go and walked over to the Porsche. He opened the passenger door. She eyed the car and then slowly walked over to it. He noticed she was limping a little.

"Is your leg okay?" he asked.

"Just some minor muscle damage, riding makes it act up a little," she said. "You were telling me where we are going for breakfast."

"It's a surprise," he said.

"Um…in Royal?" she asked. "Is that even possible?"

"I don't mean you've never been there," he said. "Just that you don't know where we are going."

"I'll give you that," she said.

He closed the door and went around to get behind the wheel. She'd taken off her helmet and held it on her lap. She tossed her head and fluffed up her hair.

"Um…how do I look?" she asked.

"Gorgeous," he said.

He started the ignition and drove away from the stables. "We're going to a spot I'm thinking of buying."

"Really? Why?"

"My mom needs me to be here more often than twice a year. Her doctors suggested that her heart episodes might be a bid to get to see me more often." He didn't like the fact that she kept having them or that the doctors still hadn't been able to figure out why.

"I'm sorry to hear that. Are you a bad son?" she asked. "You two are all each other has."

"I try very hard not to be," he said. "But I'm busy working all the time and most of what I do when I'm not traveling around the state visiting sites is sit in my office in Dallas and go to meetings. I could easily do that from here if I found a reason to stay," he said.

"Your mom's not reason enough?" Macy asked, tipping her head to the side in a flirtatious manner.

"She's enough for me to come back here more often, but to really stay, I'm going to need something else." Chris would come back here all the time if he and Macy were dating. He wanted to see more of her. When he looked at her now, he wanted her so badly he could hardly think.

"Like a woman to spend your time with?" Macy asked.

"Depends on the woman," he said, signaling then following a dirt road down off the main highway. He stopped the Porsche and laughed.

"What's so funny?" she asked.

"I wanted to impress you with my car, but the Range Rover is better suited for this kind of driving. I should have thought ahead and brought that vehicle instead," he said. But lots of people in Royal had Range Rovers and not that many had Porsches, so he'd chosen his flashy car instead.

"Why did you want to impress me?" she asked. "I'm not judging you."

He shrugged. Chris had always been very competitive, so even if he were only competing against himself he was playing to win. And of course, if he happened to impress Macy so much the better; he wanted her to see only good things when she thought of him.

"Being with you sometimes makes me feel like I did back in high school," he said.

"How did you feel?" she asked.

"Like I didn't have enough money for you…like I wasn't good enough. And I guess a part of me wants you to know that I have plenty now."

She reached across the gearshift and put her hand on his thigh. "Chris, you were always good enough for me. Just you. I don't need fancy cars or big houses."

"Hell," he said. He wasn't able to think with her hand on his leg so close to this groin. He leaned across the seat and kissed her. Put his hands on her shoulders and drew her closer to him. Her mouth opened under his and her fingers dug into his thigh. He sat her back down and then undid his seat belt and opened his door.

"Where are you going?" she asked.

"To get some fresh air. You go to my head, Macy. Make me wish for things that I hadn't even thought mattered. I have always just focused on making money and proving to the people of Royal that I wasn't just an oil worker's son."

"You've done that a million times over," Macy said.

"But it doesn't mean anything if I still don't feel good enough for you."

He got out of the car and closed the door. Looking at the land he'd thought of buying. As a boy he'd never thought of having anything in Royal, and now because of Macy he was seriously considering something he'd never entertained before.

Five

Macy followed Chris away from the dirt road and up a small hill to a copse of trees. He had a blanket under one arm and the picnic basket in the other. She took the blanket from him and spread it on the ground.

"I like this place," she said. "It reminds me a lot of Daddy's ranch."

"Mmm, hmm."

Okay, she guessed he still wasn't ready to talk. What had she done to make him think he had to prove himself to her?

She was afraid to say anything to him. She really didn't know what to think about his comments. And she wanted to say the right thing. She was flattered... because he was trying so hard to prove himself. To show her that he had as much money as her family did.

She sort of understood what he meant. That was what riding had given her. It had been her way of proving to herself that she wasn't as badly injured as she had been.

"Do you think we ever stop trying to prove ourselves?" she asked. "I know that I fight daily with my dad because he still treats me like I'm twelve. I get that I was in a serious accident, but I've recovered now. It's about time for him to treat me like an adult."

He shook his head. "I don't know. There always seems to be another goal lurking on the horizon. Something else that I should be reaching for. No matter what I accomplish, it never fills that empty place inside me."

She reached over and took his hand. He seemed so confident and he was so successful, she thought he didn't have the same concerns that she did. But she liked the fact that they were the same in this.

"Me too. At first it was just live, then it was recover, then regain my looks, now…regain my confidence. When is it going to be enough, you know?"

"I do know," he said. He gestured for her to sit down and then placed the picnic basket near her. He sat down and leaned back against the tree. When she sat down, he drew her between his legs so that her back was resting against his chest.

He wrapped his arms around her and put his head on her shoulder and she leaned into the comfort of his embrace.

"I'm thinking of putting the main house right there."

"So you are definitely getting this property?" she asked, scooting around to face him. She didn't want to get too used to Chris. He wasn't staying here in Royal even if he bought this property. His life was always going to be in Dallas.

"Yes. I'm going to build a little house over there for

my mom," he said, pointing to the left. "I know she likes her independence, but I'd like her closer to me when I'm in town."

He was so sweet with his mom. With families so spread out now, not everyone kept close contact with their parents, and it meant something to her that Chris had.

"Why don't you buy a house in Pine Valley?" she asked, opening the picnic basket and taking out the containers. It seemed as if the upscale neighborhood would be more convenient.

"I want to build my dream home," he said, taking the thermos from her and pouring them both some coffee. The food that Maggie had prepared smelled delicious as she took it out.

"What do you want in a dream home?" she asked. What did he do in his downtime?

"Lots of things. Maybe over dinner tonight, I'll show you the plans I had drawn up."

He was so arrogant sometimes. And she wondered if she was making things just a little too easy for him, but the truth was, she wanted to see him for dinner. She liked this man she was coming to know.

"Are we having dinner?" she asked.

"I'd like to. Not out at the club, but maybe just someplace small, where I don't feel like we're in a fishbowl."

She smiled over at him. "I'd like that. My dad is going to Midland tonight for his weekly poker game. How about I cook you dinner?"

Chris crossed his arms over his chest. "That feels a bit like the sneaking around we used to do."

"I know, but I don't mean it that way," she said. "My house isn't ready for company yet."

"Why don't I meet you there," he suggested. "We can have dinner and work on *making* it ready for you."

She liked that so she nodded. "I have movers coming to get my stuff next Saturday."

"Are you hiring someone to do the work around the house?" he asked. "Did you rent it out while you lived with your dad?"

Macy shook her head. "I refused. At first it was because I didn't want to face the reality that I wasn't going to be able to go home. Then I didn't want to admit that dad had been right when he said it was going to take me time to recover."

Chris nodded at her. "I can see that. You are very stubborn."

She wriggled her eyebrows at him. Best that he know the truth about her. She never let go of something once she sunk her teeth into it. The accident had slowed her down, but she knew she was gradually coming back into her own.

"Yes, I am. It's part of my charm."

"Only part of it?" he asked with a teasing grin. She loved his smile, which was the slightest bit crooked.

"The best part of it," she said, dishing out the food. They both ate quickly, talking about books they'd read and how funny it was that they'd switched from regular books to e-readers.

"They are just so much easier to manage. Do you know I can read a book exactly where I left off at on my cell phone if I want to? My e-reader was a lifesaver during some of the long nights I spent in the hospital. If

I woke up at 2:00 a.m. and needed something to distract me, I could find a new book and download it."

"Did that happen a lot?" he asked as he cleaned up the remains of their meal.

"Yes. Some of my surgeries were painful. I did discover how much I loved some of those old classics Mrs. Kieffer assigned to us junior year."

"No way," he said, grabbing his chest as if she'd given him a heart attack. "Just playing. She picked some good books for us to read back then. Didn't you mean rediscover?"

She blushed. "I didn't read them the first time. I used to have a friend who'd read them and give me a report on what they were about."

He shook his head at her and she felt as though she'd been caught out, which she had. But back then she'd been a princess and everyone had wanted to help her. So she'd taken the easy way more than once.

"What? Not everyone likes to read. And I was busy cheerleading and sneaking out of the house to meet you."

"I'm glad you could sneak out to meet me. So what book did you discover you liked?"

"*Pride and Prejudice,* which led me to the entire Jane Austen collection. I even watched all the movies."

He shook his head. "Those are okay. I preferred *The Three Musketeers* or *The Count of Monte Cristo.*"

"Nah, I didn't even try those, but I can see where they'd appeal to you. Have you read *Pride and Prejudice?*"

"No, but my secretary has the one with zombies on her desk," Chris said.

"That's not the same, though I did read it. I'm going to lend it to you," she said.

"If you insist, but then you have to read *The Count of Monte Cristo*."

"Deal. We can chat about them next week." She was a quick reader given that all she had been doing was lying in her bed. She might not be able to finish the book as quickly now that she was working for her dad in his office.

"A week? I don't read that fast," Chris said. "I barely have time to catch a game on TV, much less read an entire book in one week."

"I used to. I might not have any time now either. Okay, then we can chat when you say you're done," she said. Today had made her feel normal. Riding was part of her old routine, and Chris, whether she wanted to admit it or not, was part of her new routine. He was a bridge between the pain-filled existence she'd had before and the present.

"Thank you for breakfast. Please tell your mom I enjoyed it," Macy said. She liked that about her small hometown. The fact that many generations still lived there and that for the most part everyone knew of everyone else.

"I'll do that. So, if we are having dinner at your place tonight, I'll need the address," he said.

She nodded and then gave it to him. Reluctantly, she said goodbye to him when he took her back to her car. He didn't try to kiss her again and she hoped he hadn't decided she wanted them to just be friends. Because she wanted so much more from Chris Richardson, more than she'd ever realized before.

* * *

Chris spent a long time at the office and then on the phone with a vendor back in Dallas for a new retail center he was developing in Plano. He rubbed the back of his neck and stood up and stretched. He'd tried not to think too much about Macy today, but his thoughts always strayed back to her.

After that kiss in the car this morning, he'd tried to lighten things up, but he couldn't loosen the knot in his gut. It was more than a knot. It was that same feeling he'd had all those years ago. He was falling for her with her quick smile and teasing ways.

"Chris, Harrison Reynolds is back. He is demanding to see you," Tanja, his administrative assistant, said from the doorway.

Tanja had close-cut hair and pretty features. She was thin and efficient and had moved here when her doctor husband had taken a job at Royal Memorial Hospital. She used to work for Chris in Dallas. He had no true need for an office here, but had opened one so he could keep her on staff.

They did all the West Texas business out of this office and he always had a place to work when he visited his mother.

"Of course he is. Will you send him to the conference room and get him a beverage?" he asked. "I'll be down there in a minute."

"Yes, sir," Tanja said. "I sent the bid for the new headquarters over to Brad Price this morning for you."

"Thank you. I need a meeting with the TCC board on the schedule too. Will you call Brad's secretary and find out when it will work for them?"

"Of course."

Chris waited until Tanja left and then stood up and paced around his desk. Why was Harrison here again? Chris was doing everything he could to look into their bidding processes. He didn't really want to talk to Macy's father. He straightened his tie and put a gracious smile on his face. No matter what transpired between him and Harrison, Macy was still going to see him for dinner tonight.

They weren't teenagers anymore and Harrison had little control over either of their actions. Maybe it was time he let Harrison know that fact in no uncertain terms. But that wasn't his way, Chris thought. He wasn't interested in talking to Harrison about Macy. That was none of the older man's business.

He pushed open the conference room door and entered quietly. Harrison was on the phone, but stood up when he heard the door.

"I'll call you back," Harrison said. "Hello, Chris. Thanks for agreeing to see me."

Chris arched an eyebrow at the older man. Who reminded him a lot of J.R. from the old television show *Dallas*. He was bullheaded and had that Texas attitude. He was going to keep on Chris until Chris gave him the answer he wanted to hear.

"I was under the impression that I didn't have an option," Chris said. "I don't have a lot of time for this meeting, Harrison."

"Sorry about that. I didn't have time to make an appointment and wait to hear back from you. Word at the Texas Cattleman's Club is you are the frontrunner for the new development and I wanted to make sure that Reynolds Construction is the prime choice to do the work." Harrison leaned back in his chair and put his booted feet on the conference table.

"Given that you are a club member, I'm sure you will be chosen by the board for the work," Chris said. The old boys' network was still alive and well in this part of the world. Something Chris had run up against a lot when he'd first started out. It was still amazing to him that now some of those good old boys wanted to do business with him.

"Good. When are you submitting the bid for the work?"

"I've already sent it over to Brad for review. The scope is pretty broad and I want to make sure I've got all the details."

"Good," Harrison said.

"I'm not sure why you're here," Chris said.

"I'm here because…well, you've turned out to be one of the best developers in the state and I don't want to let our past relationship spoil any future endeavors."

"Okay."

"That's why I'm offering to help you out at the club. I may have misjudged you, boy. Now, what's the deal with bids I've submitted to do work for your company?"

Chris shook his head. "I don't know. We are running an internal investigation and going through all the bids that you submitted to us. It's not a quick process."

"Okay, keep me posted," Harrison said.

As if he had a choice. Harrison would probably show up at his office every couple of days until he had an answer on it. The man had a huge ego. And now Harrison had decided they should forget about the fact that he'd forced Macy to break up with Chris in high school. The older man took Chris's forgiveness for granted. "I will, is that all?"

"There is one more thing," Harrison said, standing up and putting both hands on the conference room table. "But it has nothing to do with business."

"Go ahead." Chris had been expecting a warning from Harrison since he'd heard he was here.

"I heard you and Macy went riding together this morning," Harrison said. "I don't want you toying with her. It's one thing to play with me when it comes to business, but Macy is a woman and she doesn't deserve to be treated poorly as some sort of revenge from you."

Chris stood up. He was tempted to not say anything else. To let Harrison stew in his fears for Macy. But he couldn't do it. He wasn't being dishonest with Macy or Harrison about why he was here and what he was doing. "I'm not after revenge. Macy is a special lady to me and I'm not going to use her, and it's an insult to imply I might."

Harrison shook his head. "It's no insult. You and I both know you were pissed as hell at having to leave Royal without her. I just want to make sure you aren't still looking for revenge."

"If I was, it'd be on you, not Macy," Chris said, giving the older man a steely glare. "I'm not the poor boy you rode out of town, Harrison. You should keep that in mind before you make any threats to me."

Harrison held up both hands. "I didn't mean anything by that."

Harrison stared him in the eye and Chris felt the sincerity in the older man's gaze. "It wasn't personal, Richardson, I just want the best for her."

Chris could understand that. He didn't have kids

of his own, but he knew when he did, he'd probably do the same thing. That was the job of the father. "I understand. I want the best for her too. And I think she's forgotten how to let go and just enjoy her life."

"It's been a real struggle," Harrison admitted. "I had to stand back and let her do her own thing. Damn stubborn girl."

"Wonder where she gets that from," Chris said.

That surprised a laugh out of Harrison. "It's a mystery. Thank you for meeting with me. I'll wait to hear from you about the bid for the club."

Harrison shook Chris's hand and then exited the conference room. Chris just watched the older man leave. He would never have guessed he'd have anything in common with Harrison Reynolds.

It was funny how much life and maturity changed a man's perspective. He hadn't realized that love had motivated the older man.

He walked back to his office and put Harrison out of his mind, preferring to think about Macy. Tonight was going to be a special night. The date at the club was too public to be anything other than dinner, and this morning, riding was too... Well, the horses had made it impossible for them to be close. But at her home—that was where he'd have a chance to put some bonds between them that Macy would be hard pressed to undo.

Just thinking about her made him hot and hard. Ready for something that had nothing to do with revenge. And he wanted to make sure that Macy knew he was interested in her, period. There was nothing else motivating him except that pretty smile of hers and her feminine body.

The same things that had drawn him to her the

first time. This time, though, he knew that it was her strength and her intelligence that kept him coming back for more.

Macy didn't expect to feel emotional about returning to her old home, but she did. The grass was neatly trimmed and the entire landscape well cared for by the gardener she'd been paying bimonthly. From the outside it looked as if nothing had changed from the last morning when she'd left the house.

The lights were on and when she pushed the garage-door button and pulled into her garage, it was as if no time had passed. Even her flip-flops were still sitting by the door where she'd left them from a beach trip the weekend before.

The past three years melted away and she thought she'd be meeting her fiancé inside. She had a sort of double vision as she got out of her car and unlocked the door to go into the house. It smelled a little stale and not like the room fresheners she used to keep plugged in all the time.

Her home had remained unchanged, but she had changed in many ways. She flipped on the air-conditioning and slipped off her work shoes, putting on the flip-flops she'd left by the garage door. She went back to her car and started bringing in the cleaning supplies and groceries for the night's meal.

She just needed to do a light cleaning because her father had maintained a cleaning service for her while she'd been living with him. They shared the same cleaning lady, which they'd always done.

She walked through the house, which felt too quiet at first, but then when she hit the button to turn on the radio in the intercom and music from her favorite station filled the house, she started to relax. She walked through the rooms, plugging in the scent of Island Breeze and turning on ceiling fans. She left her bedroom for last and stopped in the doorway.

The bed was draped with a dustcover, as was all the furniture in the house. The dresser top had been cleared off and all the contents taken to her room at her dad's house. She turned on the light and walked inside, her eyes alighting first on the picture of her and her parents that sat on the bedside table.

As she aged, Macy saw herself becoming more like the woman in the picture. She scarcely remembered her mother. That pretty stranger holding her on her lap was more of a feeling—like being wrapped in a hug—than any real person.

The doorbell rang and she glanced at her watch. Though she'd intended to be only a few minutes walking through her two-story ranch-style home, she'd been over an hour.

She pushed the intercom button. This might not have been a good idea. She wasn't sure she wanted company while she sorted through the past that was here.

"Who is it?"

"Chris."

"I'll be right down," she said.

"Take your time."

She hurried down the stairs to the front door and opened it. Chris stood there in a business suit sans the jacket and tie. He'd rolled his sleeves up, but left his shirt tucked into his waistband, accentuating his lean waist.

"Hello," he said.

"Hey. Come on in," she said.

He crossed the threshold and handed her a bottle of wine. She led the way through the house to the kitchen. She was nervous about having him here. The little innocuous dates they'd had so far didn't really have any significance. They were the kind of dates that friends went on. But being here—totally alone with him—was different.

"I haven't started cooking yet."

"No problem. Why don't I get started on the dust-covers while you cook dinner."

"You don't mind?"

"That's why I came over. And that's a fairly simple job that doesn't require you," he said. "I'm going to grab a change of clothes from the car. Where can I get changed?"

"The hall bathroom," she said, gesturing toward the door next to the stairs. She had an open downstairs floor plan. Only the den and kitchen had a wall between them. Otherwise the dining and formal living rooms led smoothly into the family room and dine-in kitchen.

"I'll be right back."

She nodded and watched him leave. Then realized she was staring when he glanced back at her.

"Like what you see?"

She refused to be embarrassed. "Yes, I do."

The man had a nice butt and she cut herself some slack for watching him walk away. She turned quickly toward the refrigerator when he glanced over his shoulder again. She smiled to herself as a feeling of joy washed over her. It had been a long time since she'd experienced something like this.

She put a pot of water on to boil and salted it liberally.

Then set about sautéing mushrooms and some herbs, along with a couple of shallots. As she worked in the kitchen, she felt time slip away from her again.

Chris worked in the house and she heard him moving from room to room upstairs. It was comforting and homey. She hadn't realized how alone she'd been in her father's house until this moment. Her dad had his own life and had of course made time for her in it, but there had been no one to cook for or to share her evenings with.

She made a white sauce and grated some cheese and as soon as the pasta was done she mixed all the ingredients together in a casserole dish and put it in the oven to bake. She made her version of "cheaters" chocolate-mousse pie—a recipe that she'd found in her mother's cookbook. Using whipped cream and melted chocolate, she combined them and then put the combined ingredients in a cookie-crumb piecrust and piped a little cream around the outside of the crust before placing it in the refrigerator to chill.

Then she set the timer and went upstairs to find Chris. He was in her game room, standing in front of the spot where the big-screen TV used to be.

"What happened here?"

"My fiancé. He was the one who bought the TV. I guess he took it back when we broke up."

"Dirtbag," Chris said.

"I scarcely use this room," she said, making excuses for Benjamin, as she had so often when they were together. "He liked the television and I wasn't really using it."

"That's not a good reason to take it. He must not have

been much of a man to have left you while you were so sick."

"He...I guess he wasn't," she said. She walked away from Chris and he cleared his throat.

"You have a very nice house," he said.

"Thank you. I like it. I know it's too big for one person, but I always thought I'd have a family someday. And it was a good investment. My dad's company did the construction of this subdivision, so I got a good deal."

"It makes sense to me," he said. He took the last dustcover off the leather sofa and folded it quickly. He placed it on top of the pile he'd made with the other ones and then walked over to her.

"I've waited all day to do this," he said. He pulled her into his arms and slowly lowered his head. She reached up and put her hands on his shoulders.

"I've waited too," she whispered.

"Good," he said as he kissed her. The warm exhalation of his breath brushed over her and she shivered in his arms. He tasted of that feeling that evoked home. And though the smell of dust covered with Island Breeze filled the room, all she inhaled was the spicy scent of Chris's aftershave. His hands rubbed up and down her back and when he lifted his head, she snaked her arms around his waist and laid her head on his chest right above his heart.

Chris was a good man, the kind she'd always wanted for her own and, standing in this big house in the shadows of her old dreams of the future, she wished somehow their paths had been different and that this could have been their house.

Six

Chris watched Macy move around the kitchen as she prepared their dishes for dinner. He'd washed up and now sat at the counter where she'd set up two place mats. He'd opened the wine, a nice California Merlot that he ordered by the case.

"How was your day?" she asked.

"Had a visit from your dad," he said. He wasn't sure how much he wanted to say about Harrison to Macy, but he thought she should know who was still trying to run her life.

She arched both eyebrows. "Really? Was he still asking about the bids we didn't win?"

"Yes. And the bid I'm working on for the Texas Cattleman's Club," Chris said. "He's a very strong-minded man. I think he just expected me to open up my files and show him everything."

"No kidding," Macy said as she placed a plate of

steaming noodles and cheese in front of him. "Sorry it's only a casserole."

The smells were mouthwatering and, as they ate dinner and talked about the construction business in Royal, he was amazed at the normalcy of the evening. There was something so perfect about being here with Macy. She was smart, funny and had keen insights into the people in their hometown. Something she hadn't had years ago.

"You've changed," he said, realizing that she was a different woman than he'd expected her to be. Part of the transformation had to have come from the accident, but the other part he thought came from her experiences.

"Duh," she said, winking at him.

"No, I mean you seem to really understand what makes people tick. You used to only understand what motivated you."

Macy shrugged and took a sip of her wine. "I spent a lot of time home alone. Aside from reading books, I also surfed the Net and read about our town. And... promise not to tell anyone?"

"What am I promising for?" he asked.

She leaned forward. "My dirty little secret...the thing that has made me so intuitive."

"I promise," he said.

"I watch *Maury*. Once you do that, the human psyche is easy to understand."

That made him laugh. He had never watched the daytime talk show, so he couldn't really say whether or not that was a valid benchmark for human behavior. And it couldn't have surprised him more. That television show wasn't at all what he'd expected her to watch.

"What exactly did you learn from Maury?" he asked, wanting to hear her insights.

She gave him an impish smile. "One thing I love is seeing into other people's lives, especially if they are more messed up than mine. But really I learned why cheaters cheat and why family dynamics get messed up."

"Why is that?" he asked.

"They are searching for someone to love them and listen to them. The problem is that they keep going back to the same type of people. It's an endless cycle."

She was sincere and he had to agree with her. He'd certainly been drawn to the same type of woman all his life. Someone with thick honey-blond hair who was just a little bit out of his league. But in his case it had worked as a catalyst for him to keep working harder and harder until he had improved not only his circumstances but also his life. And now the woman he wanted was no longer out of his league.

"I can see that. What kind of man are you drawn to?" he asked. "Have you learned from your broken engagement?"

"I think so. I spent a lot of time dissecting it. I could see that Benjamin needed something that I could never give him," she said, sounding the tiniest bit sad.

"What was that?"

"He needed a woman who would be happy to be his trophy wife and have his kids but turn a blind eye to his mistresses. He traveled a lot for business. And I'd miss him so much, but he never seemed to mind the separations. Once we broke up, I realized I wasn't really special to him..."

"How did you realize that?" he asked. That's not

something that any woman would just recognize about a man she was going to marry.

"He told me. He only asked me to marry him because…" She paused and looked down at her hands. "This is a little hard to say."

He reached over and took her small, well-manicured hand in his. He really hated that jerk she'd been engaged to. At first it was just because she'd been engaged to him, but now it was full-on hatred because he hadn't realized what a treasure Macy was.

"I'm not going to judge you."

She swallowed hard and then took a deep breath. "I wouldn't sleep with him otherwise. I was saving myself for marriage. I know that it might sound silly, given the morals of today, but I was raised differently and I didn't want to give myself to a man who wasn't committed to me."

"So what happened?" he asked.

"Benjamin asked me to marry him and I said yes. Once we were engaged, we started sleeping together and then…the accident happened."

He stroked his thumb over the back of her knuckles and struggled to keep calm. He didn't like thinking of any man sleeping with Macy, but knowing the bastard had run out on her when she'd needed him made Chris furious.

"I understand," he said, but inside he was writhing, wishing he'd been the man she'd trusted with her virginity and who knew her heart. For Macy it was clear the two had gone together.

"Do you?" she asked. "I'm still not sure I do. The only thing I really know is that I'm mad at myself for trusting Benjamin and not seeing through his lies. Abby says it's because in the first brush of love we don't see the real man—we only see the man we want him to be."

Those words were a bit cynical, but then Abby had lost her husband unexpectedly, so Chris cut her a little slack. "Sometimes you see the real man. I'm not pretending to be anyone I'm not."

She shook her head. "It's not that the man is pretending, it's that…I fill in the missing pieces in my mind because my heart is saying he's the one. Does that make sense?"

He nodded. "I can see that. Like when an older rich man finds a pretty young wife and everyone says she's out for his money but he says she loves him and understands him."

"Exactly. And sometimes he's right, but other times he's not and there might be a bitter divorce a few years later. The hard part—and even Maury can't help me figure this out—is that I can't tell when I'm filling in the blanks and when a guy is the real deal."

He leaned over and pulled her out of her chair and onto his lap. He kissed her again and held her strongly against his chest. "I'm the real thing, Macy."

She tunneled her fingers through his hair and kissed him back with more passion than he'd expected. "I hope so."

"Why don't you see what's on TV while I clean up from dinner," she suggested.

"I was hoping to hold you," he said.

She blushed and stood up. "That would be nice."

"Then leave the dishes and come with me," he said, holding out his hand to her. She took it shyly and he realized something he should have earlier. Macy wasn't just shy about her body postsurgery, she was innocent in general. That was what that tale about her fiancé had shown him.

He settled on the couch. When she sat down, he pulled her close to his side. She curled her legs under her and leaned her head against his shoulder.

He knew of only one way to prove to Macy that he was everything she wanted and needed. And doing so would take time. The more time the better, because he had wanted to caress and kiss this woman for what felt like eons.

Chris put on the Texas Rangers baseball game. And Macy was hyperaware of him sitting next to her on the couch. She liked the way he felt pressed against her side.

After a few minutes, Chris put his hand under her chin and tilted her head back so that he could kiss her more deeply. She wanted this.

She'd always wanted more with Chris than she'd ever gotten. In high school she'd been too into herself to really think about making out, but Chris had ensured each kiss they'd shared had been hotter than the one before it.

Kissing Chris now took her one step closer to re-claiming her femininity and the woman she was becoming. His tongue tangled with hers and the kiss was passionate but not overpowering. Much like Chris himself. His lips were soft against hers and when he pulled back and looked down at her, his blue eyes were filled with passion.

"You taste...like something so irresistible, I want more," he said.

"Me too," she admitted.

"Good."

"Why didn't you kiss me when you dropped me off at my car this morning?"

He kissed her again. "I wasn't sure I wanted to let this go any further."

"Why not?"

"You broke my heart, Macy, when you dumped me. And I know it was just puppy love, but I don't want to let you do that to me again," he said.

She turned on the couch to face him and put her hands on his shoulders. "I'm so sorry, Chris. I wish...I wish I could have been someone else back then. Someone who would have seen you for the wonderful man you are today, but I wasn't."

"I don't want you to be someone else," he said. "I liked that brash, flirty girl who thought she was the center of the universe."

Macy had to laugh at the way he described her. She had been too full of herself. And life had made sure that she had learned the hard way there was more than just Macy Reynolds in it.

"Want to make out?" he asked. "We didn't really get to that much in high school and I want to put my hands on you, Macy."

"I'm not sure...I am still scarred from my accident. And I'm not very experienced. I'm sure you've had lots of experience." *Oh, my God,* she thought, *I'm rambling.* But she couldn't help it.

He ran his hands up and down her back before drawing her hips forward so they were pressed close together. He maneuvered them on the couch so that he was lying against the back and she was cradled in his arms. She wanted this and so much more.

"I knew one kiss wouldn't be enough," he said against her lips.

She shifted against him and continued kissing him as she caressed him through his T-shirt. He'd changed into a pair of khaki shorts and a T-shirt to help her clean her house.

"You feel so muscular," she said.

He laughed a bit self-consciously. "I try to work out at least once a day when I'm in Dallas. I spend so much time sitting at my desk otherwise."

She bit her lower lip as she thought that she'd really like to see what he looked like without his shirt on.

"What?"

"Um...will you take your shirt off?" she asked.

"I'd love to," he said. "But I might ask you to take yours off too."

"I'm not pretty," she said.

"No, you're not," he said. "You're gorgeous. But we can do that on your timetable and not mine."

He sat up and pulled his shirt up over his head and tossed it on the floor. His abs were solid—not a six-pack but still nice-looking.

She ran her fingers over his chest. There was a light dusting of hair on it and it tickled her fingertips as she drew them over him. She leaned forward and lowered her head to kiss his neck and shoulders while letting her hands explore his body.

She liked touching him. She realized that he seemed much more the boy she'd known like this than the tycoon who'd come back to town to prove his worth.

She felt his hands at the small of her back, slipping under her shirt and slowly pulling the material up her body. She put her hands on the waistband of the shirt and held it in place. She wondered if he thought she'd been kidding. She was scarred and she didn't want him to see her like that.

"I won't take off your shirt if you don't want me to," he said. "But I do want to touch you."

She nodded and he slipped his hands under her shirt, skimming them over her body. Finding the burn marks on her right side.

She held her breath waiting for his response to them, but he didn't say anything. As he traced the scar tissue goose bumps spread out from the spot and she shivered. "I'm sorry—"

"Don't," he said, putting his finger over her lips. "You are beautiful. Every inch of you, don't forget that."

He slid off the couch to his knees so that he was next to her. He pushed her shirt up and she watched him instead of looking at her own body. He leaned down and traced the scar with his fingers and then she felt the warm wash of his breath on that area.

A moment later she felt a soft kiss against that damaged area. The scars no longer caused her physical pain, but she hadn't realized how much she resented them until she felt Chris touching her there.

"What are you doing?" she asked.

"Healing this wound."

"Why?" she asked.

"Because I want you to know how sexy this is on your body because it's part of what has made you into the woman you are today," he said.

He lowered his head again and she put her hands on the back of it, feeling his silky blond hair under her fingers. She'd known Chris was different from the other men she'd met and dated, but until this moment she hadn't really understood why.

He shifted and took her mouth again in a sweet, passionate kiss. But she wasn't ready for more tonight. She was vulnerable and more fragile than she would have guessed. She put her hands between them, pushing gently on his shoulders. He lifted his head and looked down at her.

She could only stare into his eyes for a few long moments.

Chris got up and walked out of the living room toward the sliding glass door that led to her backyard. He opened it and the hot August heat rushed over his chest. He wanted more from Macy than she could offer him at this moment.

Plus, he didn't want to pressure her. A moment like this wasn't only going to happen once, and the next time he'd be prepared. He walked around the pool over to the built-in barbecue grill. She had everything in this house that would make it a home.

"Chris?"

"Yes?"

"Do you want a drink?" she asked, sounding a bit disjointed. "I make a mean martini."

He laughed. "Sure, I'll take one."

Her lips were still a little full from his kisses. He wanted to touch her all over again. Just run his hands over that sexy body of hers. But that was a path that would lead to more frustration.

"Actually, I think I'm going to take a rain check on that martini. I better head home now."

"Oh, okay."

He walked over to her and pulled her into his arms, holding her tightly against his chest. And she put her head right over his heart again. "I need some space to breathe or I'm going to be pushing you to make love with me. And I don't want to do that."

"You didn't push me," she said.

"I will if I stay. Are you going to be okay here if I leave?"

She nodded, her head against him. "Yes. I'm going to finish making the beds and wash the dishes, and then I think I'll head back to my dad's."

"Are you available for lunch tomorrow?" he asked.

"I think I have room in my schedule for you. What did you have in mind?"

"Maybe a trip up in my plane?" he asked. He had a small Piper aircraft that he used to commute between Dallas and Royal.

"I'd love it," she said. "I'll pack us a lunch."

"Sounds good," he said. He tilted her head and kissed her again. The embrace was full of passion. He knew he had to let her go or it would blossom into much more than kissing and petting.

But he didn't want to let her go. He liked the way she felt in his arms and letting her go was the absolute last thing he was going to do.

But when she put her hands on his hips and drew him closer to her, so that he was pressed against her thighs, he knew he had to leave.

He pulled back and slowly drew her arms down his body and held both her hands in his.

"Thank you for tonight."

"You're welcome. This might be the best date I've ever been on," she said.

"What about that picnic by the lake back when we were kids?" he asked. That date held many special memories for him.

She shook her head. "This one is better because it is happening now and I think…this time I'm not going to make the same mistakes I did before."

"I hope so," he said. He kissed her again and then walked toward the front door.

He got in the Porsche and drove out of her neighborhood at a sedate speed, but he didn't feel sedate. He felt wild and excited and like everything in his life was about to change. He drove out of town until he was on the long open highway where traffic was light and he put the pedal to the metal, driving as if he could escape the past.

Driving as if he had the answer to his future and there were no questions about himself and Macy and whether or not they really belonged together.

He knew he wasn't back here for revenge and he suspected she did too, but he was afraid that she'd bow to pressure once again to not stay with him. He may have changed on the outside, but he knew he was still the same inside—where it really counted. And as sweet and loving as Macy had seemed in his arms tonight, he also knew that she was just coming back to life after a long dormant period.

He was the first man to kiss her and touch her in three years. And if she were to be believed, only the second man in her entire life.

He started laughing out loud as he realized that once again Macy Reynolds had him tied in knots and he had no idea how to untangle them.

Seven

"Good morning, Dad," Macy said as she entered the kitchen the next morning. She gave her father a kiss on the forehead and then made herself a cup of Earl Grey tea.

"Morning. How was your night?"

"Good," she said, trying not to blush when she thought about her night with Chris. "I worked on my house getting it cleaned up and ready for me to move back in."

"You don't have to move," he said. "I'm fine with you staying here."

"Thanks, Dad. But I think I need to do this. It will make me feel like I'm getting back on my feet."

He squeezed her hand in his. "You're doing an amazing job of recovering. I always knew you had your mother's strength, and you really proved it during this ordeal."

"You always said that I did, but I never felt like it. Everything in my life was just a little too easy, with no real challenges." That might have been why she'd dated Chris. He was the first thing she'd had to work for. She'd enjoyed him, of course; he was such a cute boy back then. And he still was, but there was also the challenge of dating someone forbidden.

"I didn't want you to ever have to struggle for anything you wanted. Grandpa Reynolds didn't give me a dime and made me work twice as hard as everyone else at the construction company to prove myself. I resented my old man and I never wanted you to think of me the same way."

Macy got up and hugged her dad. "I never have. Even when you were imposing your rules about who I could and couldn't date."

He shrugged his big shoulders—the ones that she could remember sitting on and watching parades from when she was little. Her dad had been her first hero and he'd done a good job of making her feel special when she was a child. "I have always tried to protect you."

"And yet I still got hurt," she said. "Isn't life funny that way sometimes?"

No matter what her father had done to protect her, she'd still made mistakes and gotten hurt and made bad decisions, like accepting Benjamin's marriage proposal. Of course, when her dad had said he didn't like Benjamin that had only made her more determined to make the relationship last.

Harrison shrugged. "Yes, it is. All we can do is live by our own code and hope we've not hurt too many people on our journey."

"I think you do a great job of that, Dad."

"Thanks, kiddo. I've got an early-morning meeting at the club to talk about the remodeling they are doing."

"Why are you trying so hard to get that job? We don't need it," Macy said.

"I want to make sure that I'm not affected by Sebastian's misdeeds. He was a friend of mine and I was blind to what he was doing."

"No one blames you," Macy said.

"I blame myself for not catching on," Harrison said. "The club has always been my second home and I want it to continue to be."

She understood that. Her father was fiercely loyal. "Are you eating at home tonight?"

"No, I'll probably work late and stop by the club on my way home. You?"

"Not sure. I have a new book I'm reading."

Harrison laughed at her in a kindly way. Then shook his head before he said, "Girl, you live an exciting life."

She smiled at her dad and lightly hugged him. "I know. Try to keep up."

After he left, Macy finished her tea and then got dressed for work. She was looking forward to her lunch date with Chris. She'd had steamy dreams about him last night. In fact, she hoped to make those dreams a reality today.

She wanted Chris to be hers. Not just some guy from her past or a man she was casually dating. Last night went beyond casual for her.

Was she really going to let things move forward? Could she stop them? For the first time in her life she wanted a lover. Not a fiancé or a boyfriend but a lover. Well sort of. She felt a wave of something wash over her. She glanced at herself in the mirror, seeing her newly repaired face, but also finally starting to accept that the woman in there was her.

That wasn't a stranger staring back at her, but a woman who was strong and confident. A woman who had no problem attracting a sexy man like Chris Richardson.

She drove to the grocery store and picked up everything they needed for lunch and then drove to work. She spent the morning in the orderly world of numbers and formulas. A place where everything added up and no emotions were needed and she liked it. It gave her grounding to her exciting new life. The relationship with Chris was something unfamiliar but so much a part of who she was becoming.

Thinking about him distracted her from her work. But she didn't mind. For too long all she'd had was pain, and work was an escape, but now she had something more fulfilling in her life. Something that she wanted to claim for her own—a man she wanted to claim for her own.

She shut down her computer ten minutes before Chris was supposed to arrive and grabbed her picnic basket to meet him out front. Her dad hadn't said anything to her about dating Chris, but she knew after he'd interrupted their dinner at the Texas Cattleman's Club, he had to have guessed they were seeing each other.

Chris spent most of his morning on the phone with his client in Plano. He really should be focused on his bid to the Texas Cattleman's Club and getting out of Royal and back to his real life. But he was in no hurry to leave.

There was a knock on his office door as he hung up the phone.

"Your mom is here," Tanja said.

His mom eased past his assistant. "Thanks, Tanja."

"You're welcome," Tanja said as she let herself out of the office, closing the door behind her.

"Hi, Mom. What can I do for you this morning?" he asked.

"It's what I can do for you… Amanda Hasher's daughter is coming to town this weekend and I was going to invite her to have dinner with us."

"No."

"But—"

"No. No blind dates. Besides, I'm dating someone," Chris said.

"Who?"

"Macy Reynolds."

"I'm not trying to tell you what to do, darling," Margaret Richardson said, "but is that the smartest thing…?"

"Why wouldn't it be?" Chris asked. "Macy's a different woman now than she used to be."

"I hope so. Are you sure you don't want to just have dinner with Amanda's daughter?"

"Yes, I'm sure."

She sighed.

"What's the matter?"

"I'd like some grandkids. With my heart being the way it is…"

"There's nothing wrong with your heart," Chris said, because he wanted her to start believing that. He wanted his mother to know that he was going to be here for her even if she was healthy, but there was no way to say that.

"The doctors don't know what's the matter with me," she said, giving him her most pitiful look, and if she wasn't a master of manipulation he might have fallen for it, but he'd grown up seeing that look.

"You're right, they don't. But I'm thinking of buying my own place here so I can visit more often...that will probably help," he said, leaning over to kiss her on the cheek. He hugged her and she hugged him back.

"I'm sure it will. If you won't go out with anyone but Macy, then you can both come to my house for dinner."

"Why?" Chris asked.

"I want to see if she's sincere. Macy asked me to work on a project for her and I'd like to see the two of you together."

He shook his head and fought not to roll his eyes. "I'll ask her. But I am working nonstop on this project for the Texas Cattleman's Club and I might not be able to have dinner at a decent hour."

"Great. I will have to figure out what to make. Do you need me to do anything for you today? Dry cleaning or any of that?"

"No, Mom. You just got out of the hospital a few days ago. Shouldn't you be taking it easy?" he asked her. But it was refreshing to see her up and moving around.

"Not at all. Having you home always makes me feel refreshed."

She gave him a kiss. "I'll get out of your hair now. I'm so happy you are home, Chris. I can't tell you how much it means to me that I can stop by your office and see you whenever I want."

She left his office like the whirlwind she was and he

heard Tanja laughing at something his mom said in the outer office. He remembered how desperately he had wanted to get out of Royal, but lately his feelings about the town had changed.

Tanja poked her head back in the doorway. "Chris, I just got the files back from the head office in Dallas on the Reynolds Construction bids. What do you want me to do with them?"

"Go through the ones they submitted and find out who the winning construction company was and then look to see if we awarded to the lowest bid and if there were any special circumstances…like it was a female- or minority-owned business. Also check if there was a specific need of the original bid we did," Chris said.

"Okay. It's going to take me a little while. They've been submitting bids for the past five years," Tanja said.

"Make it a priority. I need to get some answers back to Harrison Reynolds as soon as I can. I'm taking the afternoon off. I'll have my cell phone with me, so you can get me that way if you need me."

"Sounds good. I'll just be working on this project," she said, gesturing to the stack of bids from Harrison's company.

"Thanks, Tanja," he said as she left his office.

He called the airport to make sure that Buck, who managed his private plane, had it stocked with champagne and a few other essentials. He wanted to show Macy all the things that he could give her.

Shaking his head, he stood up and paced around his office. He wasn't about to try to prove himself to her, was he? Why did he keep coming back to this?

His phone rang and he glanced at the caller ID to see it was his college roommate Sam Winston. Sam had come to UT Austin from the Northeast on a football scholarship like Chris. The two of them had become good friends and had stayed close even after they'd graduated. Though it had been a couple of weeks since they had spoken.

"Hey, Sam."

"Chris, man, what's up? I'm in Fort Worth for a conference and I called your office, but they said you weren't here," Sam said.

"I'm back in Royal. My mom was in the hospital."

"Is she okay?" Sam asked.

"Yes. That heart thing the doctors can't figure out," Chris said, catching his friend up on her situation.

"How long are you there? My conference goes until Friday and I can hang out this weekend. Georgia is having a girlfriends-only spa weekend."

"And she told you to stay out of the house?" Chris asked. He'd been the best man at Sam's wedding and he loved Georgia like a sister. She was the only one who knew how to get around Sam.

"Something like that. Are you going to leave me hanging?" Sam asked.

"I'm not going to be in Dallas this weekend. But why don't you come down to Royal?" Chris suggested.

"I could do that. Can I drive?"

"I'll send my private plane to get you. You remember Buck, right?"

"Yes, I do. Great. So I'll be down there on Saturday morning."

"Good. I'm looking forward to seeing you."

He hung up. He wanted the kind of relationship that Sam and Georgia had. They were married but didn't have to be in each other's pockets all the time. And they were happy even after five years of marriage.

That happiness had eluded Chris no matter how many different women he'd pursued. To be fair, he'd only met one woman who had made him want to put his work on hold, and that was Macy.

Maybe that was why being with her felt so different to him. He didn't know. Didn't question it anymore. He wasn't really an introspective guy. He knew what he wanted—Macy Reynolds, and he knew he was going to do whatever he had to to ensure he got her.

He'd been playing his cards close to his vest, afraid to startle Macy and make her retreat, but he was beginning to think that she wasn't running away from him; in fact, the opposite was true.

Macy had a great time at lunch, but they were interrupted by a call from her father about an hour into it. She'd had to ask Chris to take her back to Royal, which he'd done reluctantly.

"I'm sorry."

"It's fine. I know you have to be there when your dad calls."

"Not all the time, but today he needs me," she said. Though privately she wondered why he needed her now, when this morning he'd said the bid they were working on wasn't going in until Friday.

"We can have a more leisurely meal later. Are you free tonight?" he asked.

"Yes. Do you want to go out?" she asked.

"I do. Somewhere we can dance so I can hold you all night."

"Sounds good to me. I can't wear heels the way I used to," she said.

"That's fine with me."

She shook her head. "I was just thinking I wanted to look nice, sorry for blurting that out."

"You always look pretty. What do shoes have to do with that?" he asked as he drove her back to her office.

"They make my legs look longer."

"Macy, if your legs were any longer I'd die. Really, they are terrific whatever shoes you wear."

He might think so, but now that they were dating again old desires were coming back. Desires for things she hadn't thought of since she'd been in the accident. And one of them was that she wanted to put on a slinky dress and some heels.

She thought of little Sara who would be happy to wear anything closely resembling fashion and felt ashamed of herself. She'd grown beyond looks and clothing. "Thank you, Chris."

"For what?"

"Those nice things you said. I was thinking like pre-accident Macy. How shallow was I?"

"Not shallow at all. You were just used to looking at the world in a different way. That's all changed now. Don't get me wrong, I'd love to see you in whatever you think makes you look nice. I like how you were much more confident in your riding clothes than you are in your work clothes," he said. "You walked around the stables like you had the confidence of a hundred women."

His words made sense. But then Chris always seemed to. She had noticed that her clothing made her feel differently. Her riding gear made her feel confident.

She leaned over and kissed him. Nothing passionate, just a little brush of her lips against his suntanned cheek. He was more than a man from her past. More than a man she was dating and who made her feel like a woman again. More than a man she felt casual about. She was falling for him again and she didn't know if she could trust that feeling.

She'd been through so much and he was the first man she'd gone out with after her surgery. She needed to talk to someone; she needed a second opinion. Yet there wasn't really anyone she wanted to trust with these new feelings.

But then, who could tell her what was in her heart? Love wasn't like the numbers she ran in Excel for Reynolds Construction. Love didn't have any guarantees or come with promises. Love gave her this incredible feeling inside, and riding tandem with that were all the doubts and fears she'd never thought to have.

Chris stared at her and she realized she'd let the conversation lag. What had they been talking about? Riding?

"I love riding," she said.

"I could tell."

"Um…do you have plans for Saturday? I'm going over to your mom's house to work on some outfits for my Burn Unit charity. And I'm not sure she likes me."

"I do have plans. My college roommate is in town… Why aren't you sure about my mom?"

"I broke your heart years ago and she knows it. She's helping out with the charity, but she's so cool to me."

"Be yourself and she'll warm up to you," Chris said.

Maybe taking a break from seeing each other every day was a good idea. It would give her a chance to regain her perspective. She needed to make sure that what she thought she felt…love…damn, she hadn't planned on letting any man make her feel anything again. When he'd left, Benjamin had torn her heart into pieces and foolishly she'd thought that meant she'd never have to worry about falling in love again.

That was what scared her. If she let herself care too much for Chris and this was just something temporary for him—he didn't even live in Royal—how was she going to survive?

She wasn't interested in having her heart broken again. She wanted to be cautious and protect herself from the emotions he drew from her so effortlessly, but she knew it was too late. Chris had cast a spell on her whether he'd intended to or not and she wanted him not just in her bed but also in her life.

And that felt foolish to her because her dad didn't really know they were dating. And she'd just come out of a long dark period in her life. But she couldn't stop the feelings she had, and she didn't want to.

Eight

Two days later Macy was still avoiding talking to anyone about Chris. That included Abby, who had called her several times. But Macy just wasn't ready to chat. As she hit Ignore on the cell phone yet again, she heard a rap at her door. She glanced up to see Abby standing there with her phone in hand.

"I can't believe you aren't at least going to answer my call," Abby said.

Macy felt her face get hot. "I am…"

"Avoiding me," Abby said.

"Come in and close my door and I will tell you," Macy said.

Abby did as Macy asked, but instead of sitting in one of the guest chairs, she perched on the edge of Macy's desk.

"Okay, spill, what's so important you don't have time for your good friend anymore."

"I've been dating Chris Richardson."

"The developer?" Abby asked.

"Yes."

"Damn it. I wish I'd known that. I'm bringing another developer to town so that everyone knows I'm serious about my bid to be president."

"Oh," Macy said. "I guess competition is good."

"Of course it is, but I aim to win this and that means Chris might not be in town as long as you'd like him to be," Abby said.

Macy wasn't worried about club business interfering in her life. "Chris and I have some history. I really needed to talk about this, but I didn't know what to say."

"Good thing I decided to stop by and check up on you," Abby said. "Let's get out of this office and go for a walk. You can tell me all about it."

Macy saved her work and then left the office with her friend. There was a large park with several shade trees planted and a pond at the center of it near the Richardson Construction Company main offices. The two women went over there to walk and talk.

"What's up?"

"Chris and I dated briefly in high school, but my dad didn't think he was good enough for me and pressured me to break up with him, which I did."

"I think I remember hearing something about that back in school. But you've never mentioned anything about it," Abby said.

"It was high school and lately I've had something else to talk about."

"Agreed. Let me say once again how happy I am that you have no more surgeries to go through."

"Thanks," Macy said.

"Does your dad object to you dating Chris now?" Abby asked. "I don't see what his grounds would be. I looked Richardson up on the internet and he's very successful."

"I have no idea how my dad feels," Macy said. The hot August morning was starting to make her feel a little sweaty. "I haven't said anything to him about it."

"Why not? Are you afraid to?" Abby asked.

"I don't know. Maybe. It wasn't like there was an official let's-start-dating-again discussion. We just started doing things together and it keeps getting more serious… I think I'm falling for him," Macy said. "I feel like it's too soon after my surgery. What if the emotions are some sort of mirage?"

Abby wrapped her arm around Macy's shoulders, hugging her close for just a minute. "You're grown, so anything your dad says would be moot, but if you think you're sneaking around then I'd clear the air and tell him that you have been dating Chris and intend to continue.

"As for the other…love, only time will tell."

"I'm used to finding answers and plotting and planning things, Abby."

Abby hugged her again. "I know, but real life isn't like that."

Macy was more than aware that her friend was right. She needed to remember that she could plan to her heart's content and still unexpected things were going to occur. She could either go in this new direction with Chris or stop it now and keep herself from being hurt again.

"I'm afraid of getting hurt," Macy said. "I told myself

I was well rid of Benjamin, but sometimes the hurt creeps up on me and I find myself aching again."

"Trust isn't something that comes easy to any of us," Abby said.

"Girl, I thought you had all the answers," Macy said. "Don't tell me you have doubts like the rest of us mortals."

Abby shook her head. "I don't want to tarnish my image."

"You haven't," Macy said. "Thanks for making me talk to you."

"No problem," Abby said.

"Do you fancy helping me out at the children's Burn Unit on Sunday?"

"Sure, what are we doing?" Abby asked.

"A little fashionista day for my friends there. Chris's mom is making some clothes for them to wear from burn-scar-friendly material and I have some ladies from a local spa coming to paint the kids' nails, but I could use some help getting them all dressed up."

"Sounds like fun. What time?" Abby asked.

Macy gave her friend the details as they walked back to the office. And as Abby was getting ready to leave, Macy realized she'd never properly said thank-you to this woman who'd helped her through the darkest period of her life.

"Thanks, Abby."

"You're welcome, but for what?"

"Making sure I was never alone, even when that was all I wanted to be. I don't think you realize what a lifesaver you were."

"You helped me out too, Mace, gave me someone other than myself to think about," Abby said.

"Good," Macy said, hugging her friend and then going back into the office. She saw her dad sitting at his desk on the phone as usual and she hesitated for a moment, contemplating going in to talk to him about Chris. In the end she decided not to. Not yet.

On Saturday morning, as he headed out to meet Sam at the airport, Chris realized that he hadn't seen Macy in almost three days. Was she avoiding him?

Or like him had she simply gotten too busy to keep up with dating? Chris had been busier than he'd expected and had to focus all his energy on the Plano retail facility he'd been working on. They'd run into some snags with the zoning commission and no matter how much talking he did on the phone, no one was willing to speed the process along.

He picked Sam up.

"I'm starving."

"Good. I'll take you to the Royal Diner so you can get something to eat and I can introduce you to my hometown."

"At a diner?"

"Trust me, you'll know more about everyone in a manner of minutes then if you'd lived here your entire life," Chris said.

Sam laughed. They chatted about the conference Sam had been at in Fort Worth, and when they were seated at the diner, Sam caught Chris up on what he and Georgia had been doing around their house all summer. They were having a new pool built.

"Why didn't you ask me to help?"

"Your business is based in Texas. I doubt you could have found a construction crew to come to Connecticut."

"You are probably right."

They both ordered a heavy greasy breakfast of eggs and all the trimmings from a waitress that reminded Chris of Flo, the character from the old television show *Alice*. She had reddish hair that was clearly dyed and wore it in an old-fashioned-looking beehive. She wore bright blue eye shadow and was never without a piece of gum in her mouth.

She was friendly and sweet but a real character.

"Why did you ever leave this place?"

Chris had never talked much about Royal in college. "A girl broke my heart."

"You? I've never known you to let anyone get close enough to do that," Sam said.

"I tend not to make the same mistakes twice," he said. Then privately wondered what he was doing with Macy now. He had no guarantees that she wasn't going to put him through the wringer emotionally again.

"What happened?" Sam asked.

"Her dad didn't approve of me, so she broke up with me. I graduated and left for college. I never looked back."

"If only it were that simple."

"If only. Nothing ever is."

"That's so true. What really happened?" Sam asked.

"That's the truth except for me moving on so easily. I didn't let anyone close because of her and her dad. When I was young, I had this plan to come back here and show them both how successful I'd become. She'd of course beg me to take her back and I'd say no way."

Sam shook his head. "That's a nice fantasy."

"You have no idea. But reality is different. The girl... well, I'm dating her now."

"You are? What about the father?"

"He doesn't know. Isn't that crazy? I'm thirty-two and I'm still not entirely comfortable with her dad."

"Complicated," Sam said. "Things were much easier with Georgia and I. I told her we were in love and going to be happy the rest of our lives and she agreed."

"Liar. You screwed up with her and had to go and beg to get her back. Don't forget who was at your side while you did all that."

Sam chuckled again. "I have started to remember the story differently... I wanted to see you today to tell you that Georgia is pregnant. I'm going to be a father."

Chris was floored and so damn happy for his friend. "Congratulations. I can't believe it."

"We can't either. We'd just about given up on ever having any kids when this happened. Georgia's calling the baby our little miracle, and I told her she has to stop saying how I begged her to marry me...what if I have a son? He's going to want to think his dad was always a great guy."

"You are a great guy, Sam. And you are going to make a really good father. When is the baby due?" Chris asked. Sharing in his friend's happiness made him realize he wanted that too.

"February," Sam said. "We want you to be the god-father."

"I'd be honored. I'll clear my calendar so I can fly up as soon as your baby is born. I can't believe you are going to be a dad."

"Me neither. But it's what Georgia and I have been wanting for a long time. Finding each other, well, Georgia says we were lucky, and I know we were. We've always been sort of yin and yang to each other, but having a child is adding something new to our relationship. I can't explain it."

"You don't have to," Chris said.

They spent the rest of the day in Royal at the Texas Cattleman's Club hanging out and playing poker in one of the rooms. Chris sent a text to Zeke and Brad and they both joined him and Sam for an afternoon of reminiscing about college days and their football glory.

Chris felt more at ease in the club this time. Being with his college-football buddies reminded him that outside of Royal he'd found his place and he'd figured out where he fit in. Coming back here had awakened old fears and attitudes in him.

Maybe his worry that Macy was going to do the same thing to him this time as she'd done in the past was unfounded. She and her father were close, but they were all adults now. Something that was easy to forget since he'd returned home.

He broke even by the end of the night and realized he'd drunk a little too much. But so had the other guys. He and Sam called a cab to take them back to his mom's house.

They tried to be quiet when they entered his mother's house, and were successful. The entire evening was fun, but as Chris lay in his bed drifting off to sleep all he could think about was Macy and how much he wanted her in his arms.

After church on Sunday, Macy and Mrs. Richardson walked into the open play area in the Burn Unit carrying boxes filled with shoes and costume jewelry and found Sara waiting. The little girl had a radiant smile on her face. Next to her was a girl that Macy hadn't met before. She had bandages on the right side of her neck and arm.

"Hi, Miss Macy," Sara said.

"Good morning, Sara. How are you feeling today?"

"Great. I'm going home tomorrow. This is my friend Jen. I'm going to come back and visit her like you do with me," Sara said.

Macy hugged Sara and smiled over at Jen. "I have a surprise for you today."

"What is it?" Sara asked.

"A little fashion makeover," Macy said. Margaret stood beside her with her arms loaded down with clothing in every color of the rainbow.

"Yay!" Sara said. "What can I do to help?"

"Tell Dr. Webb that we are here. And then just get all the girls together and we can get started on our day of fun."

"Come on, Jen," Sara said, taking her new friend by the hand and leading her to the nurses' station.

"Let me help you with that, Mrs. Richardson," Macy said.

"Thanks. By the way, I asked Chris and his friend Sam to help out as well."

"And here I am. Where do you want this stuff, Mom?" Chris asked from the doorway. He held a long metal stand with a bar on it for hanging all the clothes.

Macy was surprised to see him. She hadn't expected him to want to spend his Sunday in the children's ward of the hospital.

"I don't know…. Macy is in charge," Margaret said. "I'm going to get the rest of the things."

Macy took the pile of clothes from Margaret and turned to look at Chris. "Put it over there."

He did as she directed and she brought the clothing over to hang it up. The main difference in the clothes that Margaret had made for the girls and normal clothing was that the garments were made with no inside seams or zippers, which could rub against sensitive skin.

Chris tipped her chin up when she was done hanging the clothes and leaned down to whisper in her ear. "I've missed you."

She'd missed him too. And seeing him again this morning made all the feelings that she'd been so unsure about come rushing back. "Me too. Did you have fun with your friend yesterday?"

"Yes. I did. You can meet him later. He's going to drop by once he wakes up."

"That will be nice," Macy said.

"Come and help me with this load, Chris," Margaret said as she walked back into the room.

Chris went to help his mom and Macy didn't have time to think about Chris or falling in love for a long time. She had little girls to help get dressed up, and tiny, sometimes bandaged feet, to put in oversize shoes.

The day sped by and Macy was surprised that Chris stayed the entire time. She'd catch him staring at her and he'd just wink before he looked away from her.

She basked in the attention from him. She liked the fact that he couldn't keep his eyes off her. And seeing the joy on the little girls' faces just made her even happier.

She felt as if everything in her life had happened for a reason, even that horrible accident. She'd never have taken the time to do something like this before. But this donation of her time was more valuable and rewarding than she'd ever expected it to be.

Abby showed up midway through the morning. "We need to talk."

"Can it wait just a few more minutes? I have one more girl to dress and then the girls are going to do a runway show for us," Macy said.

"Yes, but I heard something important and…we need to talk," Abby said.

"Okay. We will as soon as this is over?"

"Yes," Abby said. There was something about Abby's demeanor that worried Macy. But she didn't let that dampen her mood. The parents of the kids in the Burn Unit were all seated near the red carpet that had been placed on the floor.

Chris had disappeared and she realized she hadn't seen him since everyone had shown up.

"I think we are ready to start the show," Macy said.

"Not yet," Margaret said. "We have a surprise for you."

"What is it?" Macy asked.

"Boys. The girls are going to need escorts on the runway," Margaret said.

All the little boys in the unit were dressed in oversize tuxedo jackets. Underneath, many of them wore their hospital jammies, but they looked wonderful to her.

"How did you do this?" she asked.

"Chris took care of it," Margaret said.

She smiled over and mouthed the word *thanks* at Chris as came back into the room. He just nodded and went to stand behind the parents seated in the chairs. Macy stepped behind the curtain that had been hung so that the parents couldn't see the kids until they stepped out on the runway.

"Is everyone ready?" she asked.

A chorus of yeses filled the air.

Macy stepped out from behind the curtain and looked at all the parents eagerly awaiting their kids. "Thank you for coming to the Royal Memorial Hospital August Fashion Show."

She glanced behind the curtain at Margaret, who pressed Play to start the music. Macy acted as the emcee introducing each girl and her escort as they came out. The afternoon was a huge success and after the event many parents came up to her to say thanks.

Macy was moved by how happy the girls were. Abby waited for her in the hallway though and she knew she needed to go and talk to her friend. As soon as she could, she made her way over to Abby.

"What's up?"

"I heard a piece of gossip this morning at the Royal Diner…"

"About me?" she asked.

"Sort of. I don't know if there is any truth to it, so I'm not sure I should even mention it."

"Just say it. I will consider the source. What did you hear?"

"I heard that Chris is back here for revenge. That he's planning on making you fall in love with him and then dumping you the way you dumped him."

Nine

Abby's source—the Royal Diner—was not surprising. It was the place to hear gossip. Macy felt as if she'd taken a blow to the stomach. She had no idea what she was going to do.

Abby looked mad, and Macy wished she could latch on to the anger instead of feeling this horrible pain inside.

"Thanks for telling me." Her voice sounded weird to her own ears. She was starting to fall for Chris, and the man she knew wouldn't come back here for revenge. Still, she knew she was never going to be able to go back in the room and act as if nothing was wrong.

"I'm sorry to be the one to tell you this, but I didn't want you to hear this from someone else," Abby said.

"What else did he say?"

"I don't know what else was said. One of the waitresses overheard him and his friend talking and she had to refill someone's coffee, but I thought you should know."

Yes, she should know.

"What are you going to do?"

"Talk to him about it," she said. The accident had taught her that life could end in a moment. She knew how lucky she was to be alive and, honestly, if Chris was the type of man who'd think about doing something like that—then he wasn't the man she was falling for.

That man…well, he was the guy who'd brought tux jackets for the boys today and who cleared his schedule to take her flying even though he probably should have been schmoozing someone from the club to make sure he got the job developing the new headquarters.

"Do you want me to come with you when you talk to him?" Abby asked, holding her hand.

"No, it's okay. I have to do this on my own," Macy said. She had been regaining her confidence with all the dates she'd been on with Chris and just getting out of the house and reclaiming her life. She'd take care of Chris. Confront him and find out if there was any truth to the rumors.

"I'll make sure he doesn't get the job at the club when I become president," Abby said.

"No," Macy said. "Revenge isn't good for anyone. I don't want to disrupt his business. If he feels he needs to get back at me for something that happened almost fourteen years ago, then he's not the kind of man I want in my life."

"That's so true," Abby said.

Macy gave her a forced half smile. She didn't want to think that she had lousy taste in men. She'd kind of always thought that Chris was a good man. And had blamed their problems on her dad. Which made a certain kind of sense, given that she'd been easily influenced by Harrison back then.

"You know I broke up with him so my dad would give me a convertible?"

"Oh, honey," Abby said.

"That's the kind of girl I was. A part of me wouldn't blame him for wanting some kind of revenge, but I'm not like that anymore. I thought he of all people would realize it."

Abby rubbed Macy's arm comfortingly. "The information came from the diner, so who knows what part of it is true."

"There's nothing for it except to ask him and find out what he was thinking," Macy said. She could run over it in her mind a million times, but she wasn't going to be any closer to finding the answers she wanted.

Only Chris could give them to her. She still had to finish up the reception with the parents and then clean up the room they'd used. The last thing she wanted to do was confront him.

She shivered a little thinking about the time they'd spent together, the kisses they'd shared. She'd thought he was being noble, but now everything took on a more sinister meaning.

She turned red, felt her face heating up. Was Chris capable of doing all the things he'd done since they met just to lead her into a trap?

She really hoped not, but hoping wasn't going to do anything. She knew that from her time in the hospital. She had to take action and, even if it was painful, that was what she was going to do. "I'll just ask him straight up if he's here for that. It doesn't seem like something he'd do. I mean, he helped out today without me even asking."

But if his plan had been to lure her into falling for him, she guessed he would do whatever he had to in order to make her feel as if he was doing something that was just for her. She was confused and knew she probably seemed…she had no idea what Abby was thinking.

Probably pitying her because she was once again in a situation where she was—what? Macy had no idea. She was embarrassed that Abby had heard this about her. But grateful that her friend had the courage to tell her.

Abby shrugged. "I have no idea what he's capable of."

"What who is capable of?" Chris asked, coming out into the hallway.

"You," Macy said.

"Call me later," Abby said as she walked by Chris.

Standing there in front of Chris, she searched for the words to ask him if he'd done what Abby had said. But she really couldn't find them. In her head she knew what she had to say, but opening her mouth and asking him if he'd come back here for revenge wasn't easy.

"Macy?"

He sounded sincere and caring and a part of her wanted to believe everything she thought was true about him, but another part of her knew better. She'd been deceived before, agreeing to marry a man because he told her pretty lies. And then when she'd needed him, Benjamin had run away. Now it seemed that Chris, whom she'd thought was different, was cut from the same cloth. That was the part that hurt the most.

* * *

"What's going on?" he asked. Chris knew something was wrong the minute he'd stepped into the hallway and seen the women standing together.

"I'm not sure how to say this."

"Say what? I'm sorry I didn't ask you about the stuff for the boys before I did it, but I thought it would be nice to include them."

She shook her head. "Of course that's fine. I'm sorry I didn't think of it myself. You were so right to do it. Next time I put together a fashion show I'm going to get your mom to make jackets for the boys."

"I know she'll love it. She had such a good time working on the dresses," he said. "But that's not what has you upset. Tell me what's going on."

Chris reached out to touch her shoulder and Macy stepped back, away from him.

"I… Abby heard some gossip at the Royal Diner."

"Not exactly surprising. Did it involve us?"

"Yes," she said. But still didn't go into detail. She wrapped her arms around her waist and hunched into herself.

Whatever was said, it had distressed Macy, and Chris was mad enough that when he found out what was going on, he was going to go to the diner and have a word with whomever was talking about Macy. She didn't need to hear things about herself in the rumor mill. She'd worked hard to recover from an accident that would have sidelined many other people.

"What was said about you?" he asked.

"It was about you and me," she said.

"I have to know what was said," he told her. "I can't tell you if it's true or not unless you open up about it."

She took a deep breath. "Word around the Royal Diner is that you are back here to make me fall in love with you and then break my heart," she said.

Chris shook his head. Dammit, he never said that. Then he remembered his conversation with Sam yesterday morning. Obviously, whoever was listening had only heard part of the conversation. Surely Macy didn't really think he'd do something like that.

"Do you believe that?" he asked.

"Did you say it?" she asked.

"I did."

"Is it true? Why would you do something like that?" she asked. "I trusted you."

"Would you believe me if I said I was talking about the past."

"Is that true? Or have I fooled myself into thinking you are a different kind of man than you really are?"

"No. Hell, no," Chris said, pulling her into his arms. "I think what your source overheard was me telling Sam how I'd felt about you and this town when I left. It didn't take me long to figure out that what happens in high school needs to stay there. I moved on with my life and never thought of revenge again."

He hoped she'd understand where he'd been when he'd left Royal. But that boy had morphed into a man who understood that sometimes getting what he thought he'd wanted wasn't the solution to everything in life. Not getting Macy had challenged him and made him go out and achieve more than he would have otherwise.

But he had no proof to offer her other than his word and, if she didn't believe him, then he'd be in the same place he'd been almost fourteen years ago. It was funny how some patterns in his life always remained the same.

"Well, Macy?"

"Well, what?" she asked.

"Do you believe me? Do you trust your own instincts? That I'm not the kind of man who would plan for almost fourteen years to get back at a girl?"

"When you say it that way…"

"It sounds silly, doesn't it? I was a young man with a bad temper and a big ego. Hell, my own father told me you were too good for me and that I was aiming for someone I should have left alone."

"Did he?"

"Yes, I think he was afraid I'd get hurt and I did. But that doesn't mean I spent the rest of my life plotting revenge on you."

"I wouldn't have blamed you if you had," she said softly. "I broke up with you so I could get a convertible."

He shook his head. "You gave in to the pressure your father put on you. It took me about six months to realize that if I'd put up more of a fight maybe you would have stayed with me. I let you go as easily as you kicked me out of your life."

He reached for her and this time she didn't flinch out of his way. He rubbed her shoulders and then looked down into those pretty eyes of hers.

"Do you believe me?" he asked again.

"I believe you," she said.

"Good," he said, hugging her close. "I wouldn't do anything to hurt you, Macy."

He held her close and kissed her. He tried to convey in that embrace how much she meant to him. He wasn't ready to tell her how important she was to him. But seeing her today with those kids… Seeing the real heart of this woman…had him wondering if Macy was the woman he wanted to have as the mother of his children.

The woman he wanted by his side as he went forward through life. Damn. He hadn't been looking to settle down, but something about Macy made him think of family and home. Those thoughts were uncomfortable, like a too-tight tuxedo jacket, and he wanted to shrug them off.

But Macy had snuck into his affections without him even noticing and, frankly, he didn't want her to leave. He had the feeling that if he let himself fall for her, she'd be everything to him. Like Sam had said of his wife, Georgia—Macy was yin to his yang. Or yang to his yin, whichever way it went.

"I'm so glad you believe me," he said. "I don't know what I'd do if I lost you again."

She looked up at him. "Me neither. I didn't expect you, Chris. I've been on my own for a long time and I had gotten used to living a life that was one of waiting. But you make me want to get out of my shell—to take risks."

"Am I a risk?" he asked her.

"Yes, you are. When Abby told me what she'd heard…I almost didn't blame you for wanting revenge. I was so shallow back then and you said…"

Chris crossed his arms over his chest. "You broke my heart."

"I'm so sorry for that," she said. "I'm not the same woman now."

"I am coming to know that," he said.

Someone called for her. "I have to go back in there."

He watched her as she moved slowly down the hallway, hips swaying with each step she took. He wanted to pretend that he didn't want her to be his completely. To pretend that what was between them was just lust, but he knew deep inside that it was much, much more.

Macy loved the freedom of being on the back of Buttercup. Chris and she had stopped by the stables and brought the horses out to the Reynolds Ranch. Now they were riding out to the swimming hole where, as Macy recalled, they'd spent a lot of time the summer they'd been dating.

It was hot on this August afternoon, but the promise of the cool waters at the swimming hole made up for it.

"I'm sorry again for that rumor getting started," Chris said.

"It's okay. I think maybe we needed to clear the air anyway. Make sure the past is well and truly buried before we can really move on."

Macy had spent a lot of time thinking about that since Abby had told her the gossip. Living in Royal meant people were always going to know her business. She knew that everyone had gossiped about her accident, her fiancé leaving and her recovery. It was the nature of small towns to be in everyone's business and as much as she didn't like being the center of the conversation in town, she did like the fact that she always knew what her neighbors were up to.

"Abby isn't too happy with you," Macy said.

"You're the only woman whose opinion matters to me," he said.

She smiled over at him. "That is very sweet, but if you want to do business with the Texas Cattleman's

Club you have to at least consider her opinion because she is a force to be reckoned with there."

"Brad doesn't think she's going to win the election."

"I don't know if she will or not, but she is bringing another developer into the picture so you aren't the only game in town," Macy said.

"Thanks for the heads-up," Chris said. "I'm going to do what Brad asked me to do and if I can get the work then I will."

"Truly?"

"Yes. I came here for my mom and since Brad asked me to bid on the work, I thought I would, but my fortune isn't tied to the Texas Cattleman's Club."

She thought about that as they rode up to the swimming hole. Was he just making light or did the work really not mean that much to him? In Royal, the club was so exclusive and everyone wanted in. But maybe being away from Royal had given Chris a different perspective.

"Do you come out here often?" Chris asked.

She shook her head. "I mainly ride at the stables. The ranch hands shouldn't have to keep an eye out for me. They have their own work that they do."

"Why would they— Oh, when you first started riding again?" Chris asked.

Macy remembered those early days. She still had scarring and bandages on her body. The last thing she'd wanted was to see anyone. She'd hidden away from the people who worked on her father's ranch.

"Yes. I found I'm a creature of habit. Plus. it was easier to stay away from anyone who might gossip about me. I felt a bit like the Beast in *Beauty and the Beast*."

"I'm sure you were nothing like the Beast," Chris said.

"I was. No one could look right at me when I had the bandages off my face at first. I mean, the skin was trying to heal, but it wasn't pretty. Sometimes I wake up thinking that my face is still so damaged. It's scary."

"I hope that I can somehow find a way of making you forget that you ever had those scars."

"I don't want to forget," she said. "I need them to remind me of what a precious gift my life is."

"It is indeed," Chris said. They arrived at the swimming hole and dismounted.

The horses were all trained to stay when their reins were on the ground and Macy and Chris set up the picnic lunch quickly.

"I don't know about you, but I need a swim before we eat," Chris said.

"It's indelicate of me to say so, but I'm sweating," Macy said.

Chris laughed. "It looks like a healthy glow to me."

She gave him a quick kiss. She felt doubly blessed to be with him this afternoon. First, because of how sexy and attentive he was, but second because of the fear that she'd felt when she'd thought he was back in Royal for revenge.

"Thanks," she said. "Last one in has to cook dinner."

Chris stared at her for a second then said, "You're on."

Macy kicked off her boots and reached for the button at her waistband, undoing it quickly. She pushed her jeans down her legs and whipped her top and hat off at the same time, stripping down to her one-piece bathing suit in no time. She saw Chris hopping on one foot trying to get his pants and boots off at the same time as she scooted around him and ran toward the swimming hole.

His laughter followed her as she ran down the dock and jumped into the water and a second after her toes touched the water she felt Chris beside her and looked over at him as she entered the water.

"Tie," he said as he surfaced.

"I was ahead of you," she said.

"If you say so," he said.

They both treaded water and her smooth leg brushed his hairy one and she saw his pupils dilate. Suddenly it didn't really matter who'd won their little race. Chris kissed her hard and then took her hand and led her to the shallower water where he could stand up.

He pulled her into his arms and the sensation of her bathing suit against his chest was enticing. She wrapped her legs around his narrow waist and held on to his shoulders as she leaned up to kiss him once again.

She felt his hands on her butt as his mouth moved over hers. He thrust his tongue deep into her mouth, but it wasn't enough for her, she wanted more.

She tipped her head to the side to deepen the kiss and lifted her hands to his head to try to control the passion that was rising between them. But there was no controlling it and she felt more alive than she had in a long time as his hands moved over her body.

Ten

Chris felt as if it had been forever since he'd held Macy in his arms, and there was nothing he wanted more than to make her his completely. All his own doubts about her and if she'd leave him the way she had before were taken away.

It was funny that a moment so long ago could so totally define them, but it did. And he was determined to move them past it. They definitely knew each other better today than they had in the past, but that was just one area of their relationship. If pressed, he'd say they'd become good friends. And involving his mother in her project had been a nice gesture on Macy's part.

But he wanted more from her than nice gestures. What he really wanted—no, needed—was to make love to her. To bind her to him with sex and desire. Macy had other friends, but she'd had only one other lover and Chris aimed to erase that man from her memory forever.

He loosened the tie at the top of her halter-top one-piece bathing suit. The wet fabric stuck to her skin and he lowered his head and kissed her neck, rubbing his beard-stubbled cheek against her before taking one of the suit straps and tugging it down until it floated in the water. He kissed her collarbone, tasting the essence of woman and the cool water with it.

He got to the other strap and traced the outline of it with his tongue. Goose bumps spread down her arm and he wondered if her nipples had tightened from that touch of his mouth on her skin.

"Do you like my mouth on you?" he asked, nibbling at her skin while he spoke.

"I do," she said. Her voice was slightly husky and she rocked her pelvis forward so that her mound rubbed over his erection.

"Me too," he said. He put his hands on her waist and lifted her until the tops of her breasts were visible above the water. He leaned down and kissed them and then laved his tongue over the firm white globes.

He snaked his tongue out to caress first one then the other. She moaned and put her hands in his hair, rubbing his scalp as he toyed with her nipples. He straightened and brought her forward with his hands on her back and felt the tips of her breasts brush against his chest.

She arched her back. "I want more. I want to feel your mouth on me."

"My mouth has been on you," he said.

"I know, but it's not enough, Chris. I feel like I'm going to die if I can't touch you all over."

"I don't want that," he said, cupping her butt in his big hands. He rubbed her over his erection.

"Hold on to me," he said.

She tightened her legs around his hips and wrapped her arms around his shoulders. He walked toward the shore, scanning the horizon to make sure they were still alone. No one was out except them. When he got to their picnic blanket, he set her on her feet and stepped back to look at her.

Her thick blond hair was wet and clung to her face and shoulders. Her halter top was still tied under her breasts but the cups and the other strings were draped down on her stomach. He reached behind her and untied the last string of her bathing suit.

She reached for him. Touching his chest and running her fingers around his nipples. His erection hardened even more and the fabric of his swim shorts cut into him. He reached between them and pulled the front of his pants down so his manhood was free.

She gasped when she saw him naked. After a moment's hesitation, she brushed her fingers over his length, then leaned forward bending at the waist. He felt the tip of her tongue on him. He groaned her name and pushed his fingers into her wet hair, holding her to him for a minute and then pulling her up.

"I want to—"

"Not now," he said between gritted teeth. He wanted her to do that as well, but not right now. He was so close to coming and he really wanted to be inside her when he did that.

"Take off your bathing suit," he said.

She arched her eyebrow at him.

"Now," he said in his most commanding voice.

She stepped back and reached down to take it off. When she bent forward, her breasts swayed and he reached out and tweaked both of her nipples. She turned away to toss her suit on the blanket.

He put his hand on her shoulder so he could keep her from turning around and admired her from the back. There was more scarring on her back from the fire. He traced the scars with his finger, then pulled her back against his body and cradled her against him.

He was nestled between her buttocks, and his hands came around to sprawl on her flat stomach. One hand drifted lower to cover her feminine mound; the other drifted higher to tweak one of her nipples.

She shifted in his arms, her hips moving back and forth against him. He parted her nether lips and rubbed his finger lightly over them, and she turned to look at him. Lifting her mouth to his for a kiss.

He took her mouth with his as he let her turn in his arms, and he kept his finger between her legs, making sure she was hot for him. As hot as the late-August summer day. They were incendiary with each other, but he doubted they were going to last long. Even the cool water of the swimming hole hadn't dampened his desire.

He lifted her and slowly bent down until he was kneeling on the blanket and holding her in his arms. He lowered her to the blanket and she lay down on her back, spreading her legs.

He reached over her toward his jeans, which he'd tossed carelessly down, and found the condom he'd put in the back pocket earlier. He ripped open the packet while Macy reached out and cupped him in her hand. He gritted his teeth and let himself enjoy her caresses.

"Do you like that?" she asked.

"Very much."

She brought her other hand to his shaft and stroked him up and down while holding him lightly, and he knew he had to get the condom on quickly and get inside her.

He moved her hands and put the condom on. He came over her. Letting his body rub against hers. His chest over her breasts, his legs against hers and then the tip of his erection against the opening of her body.

He paused there right at the portal of her body and looked down at her. Her skin was flushed, her pretty pink nipples tight with desire and her legs sprawled wide to accommodate his hips.

He slowly entered her inch by inch, taking his time because he wanted this time to last. She caught the back of his neck and drew his head down to hers. "Take me, Chris."

Those words were the goad he needed to forget his control. He thrust hard and deep into her body; turning his head, he caught her mouth with his. Thrust his tongue deep to mirror the thrusting of his hips, and he felt her thighs shift along his and then the heels of her feet at the small of his back. She shifted herself against him. Each thrust into her body drove him closer and closer to his climax. But he didn't want to come without her. He reached between them and found her pleasure center, stroking it as he stroked her inside until she moaned low and deep in her throat and he felt her body tighten around his.

Only then did he give in and let himself come too. When he was spent, he laid his head on her breast, careful to brace his weight on his arms. She cradled him close to her naked body, her fingers toying with the hair at the nape of his neck.

He knew he should say something to her, but he had no words. He only knew that he had found the woman he'd been searching for without even realizing it. It was strange to him that it was Macy, because she was what had driven him from this place. He shifted to his side and cradled her in his arms on this hot afternoon and they both drifted to sleep.

Macy woke to the feel of Chris's mouth against hers. In the distance she heard the horses munching on grass, and a breeze stirred the leaves of the tree above them. She opened her eyes and he was right above her, his blue eyes staring down into hers. She smiled up at him.

She realized he was at her side leaning over her, his weight resting on one elbow. He traced her features with his fingertip. Now that they weren't so hot for each other she felt shy about him seeing her body. She closed her eyes as he fingered lightly over her eyebrows and down her nose. She felt his finger on the scar at the top of her lip and opened her eyes to see his reaction.

She reached for a T-shirt and started to put it on.

"You can't still be shy," he said. "Not now."

"I am. You are so perfect," she said. He was completely naked and she traced a finger over his chest.

"I'm not," he said. He took the T-shirt from her hands and sat up next to her. He traced the lines of her body.

She caught her breath at the way he watched her. It was as if he'd never seen anything as beautiful as her. She reached up, caressing his lips with her fingertips, then rolled to her side so she could see his body.

She felt as if she'd been reborn in his arms. She wasn't afraid of her femininity anymore.

She pushed him onto his back and then knelt beside him.

"What are you doing?"

"I want a chance to explore you," she said.

He propped himself up on his elbows. "Explore away."

She did. She started at his neck and shoulders, touching the strongly muscled part of his body before letting her fingers work their way down. He pulled her closer in his arms, cradling her against his chest. She lay there, just letting the peace of the moment wash over her. It had been too long since she'd experienced anything like this. She'd never felt such complete relaxation with another person.

It was odd to her that it would be with Chris Richardson.

Chris woke just as the sun was setting, waking Macy as well. They got dressed in relative silence. Though Chris had a hard time keeping his hands off her. She had changed his entire perspective today. He'd run the gamut of emotions as he'd realized the type of woman that he'd found in Macy.

He wanted to marry her and he wanted her to know that now, but he wouldn't ask her without a ring. Life was good right now and he had the time to make sure he got the right one. Macy deserved the best and that was exactly what she was going to get from him.

When they were dressed and had their spot cleaned up, he took his cell phone from his pocket and pulled her close to his side, tucking her into his shoulder, and lifted the phone to take a picture of them.

"Looks good. Will you text it to me?" she asked.

"Of course," he said. He took a minute to send it to her and then helped her onto her horse before getting onto his.

He took another picture of Macy on her horse with the breeze stirring her hair. She looked free and happy. Glancing at that picture, no one would ever guess that she'd had a life-threatening accident, and he was glad he'd come back into her life now.

When they reached the Reynolds Ranch, they called Tom, who came and picked up the horses. Macy looked tired, and as much as he wanted to spend the night with her, he knew he couldn't stay at her dad's house or have her to his mom's. He needed his own place in Royal.

"Do you have time for lunch tomorrow?"

"I think I could work you into my busy schedule," she said, smiling up at him.

"I've got a meeting in the morning at the club to discuss the new headquarters. Want to meet me there?" he asked.

"That sounds good," she said. They walked to the ranch house with its big wraparound porch. As a teenager he'd wanted nothing more than to sit on that swing with her and just hold her hand. Well, maybe a little more, but he'd have been happy with some hand-holding, but they'd never had a chance to do that.

"Thank you for everything," she said. "Your help at the fashion show yesterday really made it memorable."

He shook his head and pulled her into his arms. "I should be thanking you."

"Whatever for?"

"Having such a kind heart. Including my mom in your project gave her something to focus on instead of her health. I know you gave those kids in the Burn Unit something other than their pain to think about, and this afternoon you gave me a dream that I thought had been abandoned long ago."

She hugged him and put her head on his chest. "You gave me something special too. The entire day. I was so upset when I thought what Abby had said might be true. I never want to feel that way again."

"I don't want you to either, Macy," he said, tipping her chin up so he could see her eyes. He wanted to be sure she knew that he meant what he said from the bottom of his heart. "I promise never to hurt you."

She nodded. "I know you won't."

He lowered his head and kissed her. Held her in his arms, knowing in his heart that she was his now and he was going to get a ring and, tomorrow at lunch, he'd make it official. Ask her to marry him and then make her his wife as soon as she'd agree.

Macy Reynolds owned his heart and his soul and it was a bit silly to pretend she didn't. He wasn't ready to confess to that just yet. He wondered if he should ask Harrison for her hand.

"Does your dad know we are dating?"

"He may have his suspicions, but we haven't discussed it," she said.

"Does that mean he doesn't object?" Chris asked, pushing for an answer to the one question that really bothered him. Though Harrison had said he regretted interfering when they were younger, that didn't mean the older man would welcome him as a son-in-law.

"I honestly don't know. I'm not going to give you up, Chris. Not for anything."

"Not even a really nice car?" he teased.

She shook her head. "There is no material thing on this earth I want. And you are important to me."

"You're important to me too. I want…" He trailed off as a big Chevy half-ton pickup pulled up in the circle driveway. Harrison Reynolds got out of the truck and waved to the couple.

"Richardson? What are you doing here?" Harrison asked.

"I invited him to come out here and go for a ride," Macy said.

"Great. You are welcome to stay to dinner," Harrison said.

Chris wasn't sure he wanted to stay for the evening meal. Harrison would probably ask about the bids he hadn't won again and Chris didn't want to talk business. "As long as we don't discuss business."

"What else would we talk about?" Harrison asked.

"We could talk about my project at the Burn Unit, Dad. Don't you want to know how it turned out?"

"Of course I do, Mace. Come inside and I'll pour us some drinks."

Harrison held the door and Macy went in first, followed by Chris. He had a strange twilight zone moment as he realized he was having drinks with the very man who'd once told him to stay off his property and away from his daughter. He knew it was a long time ago, but for a second it felt just like yesterday, with Harrison holding the door.

"You okay?" Macy asked under her breath as her dad went to the wet bar.

"Fine." But he really wasn't. He didn't like being in this house with Harrison and Macy. He'd never had a comfortable time here.

"What'll you have, Macy?" Harrison asked.

"Martini, Dad. Do you want me to make it?" she said.

"Not at all. Chris?"

"The same," Chris said. Macy led the way to the big leather sofa and sat down. Chris sat next to her. Macy reached over and took his hand in hers.

Harrison glared at the two of them. Chris felt as if he was eighteen again. Chris dropped Macy's hand and stood up.

"I just remembered I have some work to finish. I better head out. Thanks for a lovely afternoon, Macy."

"You're welcome. I had a very special time."

"What was so special about it?" Harrison said.

"That I spent it with Chris," Macy said.

Harrison gave him another steely-eyed glare and Chris had the feeling that Harrison was more than ready to have him tarred and feathered.

"Walk me out?" he asked Macy.

She nodded and led the way to the door.

"Goodbye," Macy said, giving him a kiss.

"Bye," he said against her lips.

Harrison stood behind Macy, watching him. "Goodbye, sir."

"I'll see you tomorrow at the club for the development meeting, Richardson. We still have a lot to discuss," Harrison said.

Chris left with the feeling that tomorrow he and Harrison were going to be talking about a lot more than just business. And once he was on his own ground,

Chris wouldn't mind it at all. As he got in his car and drove away he shed those reservations of the past. He didn't have to kowtow to Harrison Reynolds. He was more than suitable for Macy, and Chris wasn't going to let anyone stand in the way of his having her.

Eleven

The club was packed full of past and present board members and other interested parties during the planning meeting. Chris already felt as if it was going to be a hell of a day. Abby Langley glared at him as she came into the room with some tall, thin guy with dark curly hair. He suspected that would be the candidate she was pushing for developing the new headquarters.

Brad was already seated and Chris made his way over to his friend and took a seat. "Morning."

"Glad you got here early. I just heard that Abby wants to propose someone else to do the development work," Brad said.

"I heard that last night. Any idea who it is?"

"Unfortunately for us, it's Floyd Waters. He's a member of the club," Brad said.

Chris shook his head. "I guess he's a shoo-in then?"

"Not really. A lot of the old guard isn't happy about

all the waves that Abby's making. I mean, she's only an honorary member," Brad said.

"So what do you want me to do?" Chris asked. "I could approach her and try to incorporate some of her ideas—"

"No. She's made this into a battle. She can have Floyd do her design. You and I will go ahead as we planned. I'm not worried about her or her candidate."

There was a lot of tension in Brad. Something Chris hadn't really seen in the other man before. This election at the club and the possibility of admitting women as members was making everyone here a little on edge. A part of Chris would be glad to return to Dallas where he didn't have to be involved in this intrigue.

"Okay. You should know that Harrison Reynolds will probably throw in with me to sway the vote. He is also a club member, so having the two of you on my side may be helpful."

"That's fine, but Harrison was good friends with Sebastian Hunter, so that may be why he is trying to align himself with me," Brad said.

"What did Hunter do?"

"Embezzled funds."

"Did Harrison profit from any part of the embezzling?" Chris asked. He hoped not, for Macy's sake. Surely if he did then he'd no longer be a member of the club.

"No, he didn't, but he seemed to not notice a few things that made some of the younger members question him."

Chris wasn't here to get involved in the politics, though. He'd present his development plan, talk about his past work and when it was over he'd walk away.

Work may have been the reason he first came here, but Macy and his mom were the main people tying him to Royal now. He touched his jacket pocket and felt the velvet box he'd placed in there earlier. He'd had to pull a few strings to get the local jeweler to open his shop up early this morning, but Chris was happy with the marquis-cut diamond ring he'd picked out.

Slowly a large number of women entered the meeting. All the sisters, wives and daughters of current members trailed in, and Chris shook his head. "This is going to be a long meeting."

"Damn," Brad said. "I should have made this a closed meeting."

"I don't think that would have gone over well," Chris said.

"You're right. Ready?"

"Yes," Chris said. Harrison took a seat next to him as Brad turned to his left to greet another board member.

"We need to talk after the meeting," Harrison said.

"I am supposed to have lunch with Macy."

"You can postpone it. Make it dinner instead," Harrison said.

"I'm not sure I want to do that."

"Yes, you do," Harrison said. "Now that you and Macy are dating again we need to talk."

Chris tightened his fist under the table. So the old man knew about him and Macy. And after all that had happened, Harrison still didn't approve of him. That's what that had to be about. But he had no time to worry about Harrison. He needed to focus on this meeting and on giving the best presentation he could.

A part of Chris felt as if he was on trial in front of all of Royal. Like the son of an oil rig worker wasn't good enough for the Texas Cattleman's Club. Not even for a rabble-rouser like Abby. And he hated that feeling. He'd proved himself on a much larger stage.

"Let's get this meeting started," Brad said, standing up. "Chris Richardson is here today to give us his bid on construction of the new headquarters and some additional buildings that I asked him to develop for the community."

"Before we get started, I'd like to ask for equal time for Floyd Waters," Abby said, also standing up.

"Why would we do that?" Brad asked.

"We are both candidates in this election," Abby said. "As the project won't be funded until after the voting, we should hear from both developers."

There was a lot of grumbling in the room as everyone tried to voice their opinion. Chris quickly realized that he was not going to get out of here in time for lunch. He sent Macy a text message asking if she'd meet him for dinner instead.

Sure. Is everything okay?

No, the club members are having a loud discussion, your friend Abby is stirring up trouble.

Good. TTYL.

Chris pocketed his phone and sat back in his chair waiting until the dust settled. It didn't take long for Abby to get her way, and Brad looked none too happy about it as he took his seat next to Chris again. And her developer was going to present first.

"She just keeps pushing," Brad said under his breath.

"You should be used to it by now. You've always been trying to one-up each other," Chris said.

"True enough, but it would be nice if she'd just once not argue about everything," Brad said.

Chris laughed. "No woman in Royal is ever going to do that."

"You are right, even my sister likes to argue," Brad said.

Chris didn't know Sadie very well, but he imagined she was strong-willed like her brother.

Chris listened to Floyd's ideas and presentation and had to admit they were good. When it came his turn, he did what he always did in these kinds of meetings and pushed everything from his mind except convincing everyone in the room he was the best man for the job. As he spoke, he kept in mind Harrison Reynolds and how he still thought that Chris wasn't good enough for Macy.

It was nearly lunchtime when Macy's phone rang. She hoped it was Chris telling her his meeting had ended. A lot of the other ladies of Royal were at the club observing the meeting as well. Macy had wanted to attend but had a follow-up appointment with Dr. Webb, which had turned out fine.

She had missed Chris last night and really didn't want to wait until tonight to see him. If it was Chris calling, they could still have lunch together.

"Reynolds Construction, this is Macy." She had it bad for Chris.

"Hello, dear, it's Maggie Richardson. Are you available to talk about some jacket designs I have for the boys for our next show?"

"As a matter of fact, I'm free for lunch today. Would that work for you?" Macy asked. Chris's mom had been a godsend at the last show and it was touching that his mother was ready to do another one.

"Yes, it would. I talked to Norma Jones—she's on the board at the hospital—and she would like to make your fashion show available to all the children, not just those in the Burn Unit," Maggie said.

"I like that. We can discuss it with her soon. I will try to set up a meeting," Macy said.

"I'm going to give her a call now and see if she can make it today," Maggie said.

"Okay. We can meet at the Royal Diner in forty-five minutes or so?" Macy suggested.

"That sounds good," Maggie said. "I hope I didn't overstep by instigating this meeting."

"Not at all. I think we had a great event the other day and everyone seemed to really enjoy it. I wanted to do another one," Macy said. "I have a few ideas on themes that we can use the next time."

"I can't wait to hear them," Maggie said. "I'll see you in a little while."

Macy hung up the phone thinking about how busy her life was now. She'd changed so much since her last surgery a few short weeks ago. Before that, she'd work at her home office or go riding, but that was about it. Now she was having lunch out and dating Chris. And she loved it.

She had finally gotten her life back. It wasn't the same one she'd had before and that made her happy. She continued working on the spreadsheet she was putting together and then left a little early to go to lunch. She parked her car off Main Street and walked to the diner.

But when she got there she remembered that someone in here had heard Chris talking about wanting revenge on her and she hesitated for a millisecond before reminding herself that she wasn't going to be daunted by gossip.

She put her shoulders back and walked into the diner with her head held high. She asked for a table near the window so she could see Maggie when she arrived.

Macy thought she saw one of the waitresses staring at her, and boldly Macy returned the stare until the girl walked over to her. "You look so familiar but I can't place the face, do I know you?"

"I'm not sure. I'm Macy Reynolds."

"Lucy Bell, I think we went to high school together."

"We did," Macy said. "You were on the cheer squad with me."

"I was. I just moved back to Royal."

They chatted for a few more minutes and decided to meet for drinks to catch up. Lucy was in touch with the rest of the cheerleaders and they had a weekly gabfest. Lucy invited Macy to join them the next time they met.

Lucy left when Maggie arrived. She was full of ideas. "Let's order and then I want to show you some of the sketches I did. I think I could have made the dresses better if I'd realized what kind of bandages I was dealing with," Maggie said.

"They were perfect."

Both women ordered a salad and diet cola and then started talking about fashion and clothing designs. "I think we should reach out to the parents at the Burn Unit and the patients in the cancer unit too."

"I agree, Macy. I will ask Norma for some names and numbers. Do you want me to call them?" Maggie asked.

"That would be great. I am busy at work."

"What do you do, dear?" Maggie asked.

"I'm a financial analyst for Reynolds Construction," Macy said. But then she felt embarrassed that she worked for her dad. "I used to work for a hotel chain, but after my accident…"

"No explanations are necessary. I am impressed by how much you are doing considering all you've been through."

Macy flushed at the compliment. "Look at you, just out of the hospital as well."

"It's different for me. My condition is a small heart murmur, nothing like recovering from an accident. Is it okay to mention it?"

Macy smiled kindly at the older woman. She was so earnest and blunt she reminded Macy a lot of Chris. "Yes, it is. Chris is very like you."

"Do you think so?"

"Yes, I do. He's a good man, your son," Macy said.

"I've always thought so. I hate that he lives so far away. I really miss having my son close by."

"I bet you do. Hopefully, we can come up with something to get him to come back here more often."

"We?"

"Yes, we. I want him here too," Macy said. "I know that I didn't treat Chris the way I should have in high school. But I've changed, and I really do care for your son now."

"Good. I was hoping that there was something developing between the two of you," Maggie said.

"Me too," Macy said.

The two women enjoyed the rest of their lunch and Macy realized how confident she felt, not just in herself, but also in her new relationship with Chris. It seemed as if she'd had to literally walk through fire to get to this point in her life but it was so worth it.

Chris hadn't been to a meeting this contentious before. Abby had a comment about every single stage of his development plan. He wondered if it was simply, as he and Brad had discussed, that she liked to argue, or if her attitude had anything to do with the fact that she thought he wanted revenge on one of her good friends.

Chris gave her the benefit of the doubt and tried to act as if she just wanted what was best for the club, but to his mind it seemed as though she and the other women wanted equal rights here so badly they were going to turn every decision into a battle.

Once the meeting was over, he and Brad hit the bar for a stiff drink. When Brad left, Chris had a scant minute to himself before Harrison walked up.

"What are you drinking?" the older man asked.

"Scotch neat," Chris said.

"I'll have one too...make mine a double," Harrison said to the bartender. "Let's go over there where we can talk and not be interrupted."

Chris thought about it for a minute and knew he needed to at least let Harrison know that no matter what he said, Chris was going to ask Macy to marry him. Even though he'd had enough arguing for the day, he nodded and walked over to a casual seating group made of large brown leather chairs. He sat down with his back to the door of the room.

Harrison joined him a minute later. "That was one hell of a meeting."

"I'll drink to that. After today I wonder if some of the potential members will change their minds about wanting in so badly," Chris said.

"Doubtful. Those women seem damn serious about it being their time. I liked your development ideas. You seem to know what the club needs."

"Thank you, sir," Chris said. He had thought that Harrison would jump in with his concerns about Macy, but given the long day they'd both spent talking about Texas Cattleman business, Chris guessed he shouldn't have been surprised.

"I still want in on that action."

"I know. We're not to that stage yet, but I will keep you in mind when we are."

"Good," Harrison said, sitting back in his chair. The man should have looked tired or at least a little less like a shark, but the years hadn't taken much of the starch from Harrison Reynolds. "Now, about you and Macy."

"What about us? We're both adults. I've got a good career and can definitely keep her in style.

"I heard a rumor that you only came back for revenge."

"That's not true. I told Macy this as well. What happened between the three of us was a long time ago and I'm not going to lie and say I wasn't pissed off back then, but I don't hold on to things like that. I've always been a man who looks forward to new things."

Harrison nodded. "I want to believe you, son. In fact, I do believe you, but I'm not sure Macy will."

"She does," Chris said. He was so glad that he had

heard about the rumor from Macy before Harrison confronted him. "Was that your only concern?"

"No. Even if you're not here for revenge, I know you live in Dallas. I don't want you playing fast and loose with Macy, so I'll have your word right now that you aren't going to cheat on her."

"Harrison, this entire conversation shows how little you know me. I'm not going to promise you anything," Chris said. His promises were for Macy and Macy alone. What went on between the two of them was private. He took a swallow of his scotch and then rubbed the back of his neck.

"Listen, I agreed to meet with you today and talk because I'm going to marry your daughter with or without your permission. I wanted to ensure there was no bad blood between us and I thought the best way to do that was over a drink."

"Good. I like that. If you marry Macy we can talk about merging our two companies. I like the sound of Reynolds-Richardson Builders."

"I'm not interested in merging our businesses," Chris said. He'd worked hard to have his own company and he liked being his own boss. As much as he wanted Macy in his life, he didn't want to deal with her father on a daily basis.

"I can make it hard for you two if you don't agree to my terms," Harrison said.

Chris couldn't believe what he was hearing, and Harrison was making him angry. "I'm not going to merge with you even if you offered me Macy on a silver platter."

Harrison nodded and then sat forward and motioned for Chris to lean in as well. "I can see now that you are sincere and that Macy means something to you. Do you love her?"

"I think she deserves to hear my feelings before you do. But you can trust me to take good care of her. I mean to ask her to be my wife tonight."

"I'll join you for dinner then," Harrison said.

"No. You won't. I'm going to ask her and not with an audience," Chris said. There were things he wanted to say to Macy, private things that he didn't want Harrison or anyone else to hear.

He'd never been in love with anyone before and he found he was oddly protective of her because of it. He wasn't sure what the future held and if they'd stay in Dallas or move back here, but he knew he was going to always keep an eye on Macy and keep her safe.

"Okay, but I can come over during dessert, and we haven't finished discussing a possible merger," Harrison said.

Chris rolled his eyes. Harrison was going to be an impossible father-in-law. The old man simply bullied and pushed until he got his way. "Did you do this to Macy all those years ago, just keep at her until you wore her down?"

Harrison gave him a cat-got-the-canary grin and nodded. "Hell, yes."

Chris thought it over for a minute and then finished his scotch and put the glass on the table in front of him.

"I guess if you are giving me your daughter's hand in marriage, the least we can do is talk about a merger."

"I knew you'd see it my way," Harrison said, holding out his hand for Chris to shake. "It makes good business sense and you've always been sweet on Macy, so having my approval will pave the way to your proposal and her acceptance."

There was a gasp and Chris glanced up to see Macy standing there wearing a skintight black dress with her hair up and some very sexy red lipstick on her mouth.

"Hey, babe, you look sexy tonight."

"Don't hey, babe, me."

Chris could tell Macy was upset, but for the life of him he couldn't figure out why. He thought she'd be happy he and her father were getting along.

Twelve

Macy was outraged. There was no other word for it. She'd spent the day thinking about what a great guy Chris was and then she walked into the club and heard him making some sort of bargain with her dad.

"I can't believe you two."

"What is it, honey?" her dad said.

"Calm down, Macy. Your dad and I have finally come to an understanding about you."

That made her even crazier. What was it about these men that they would use her as a pawn in their games. "I don't care what your understanding is. I'm not going to be a part of your deals. I thought you of all people would get that, Chris."

"I do, Macy."

But she wasn't listening to anything else he had to say. These men really made her so angry.

"It's not what you are thinking...what are you thinking by the way?" Chris asked.

"That my dad is offering you some kind of bribe."

"Well, that was a little negotiating on my part, Mace. Don't blame Chris."

"Dad, I'm so tired of you trying to plan my life. Didn't you see what happened to me when I thought I was on the road to a certain future? You should realize there are no guarantees."

Her dad stood up and walked over to her. "Now, listen here, girl, I'm not trying to run your life."

"You are, Dad, whether you realize it or not," Macy said. "It's partially my fault because I let you give me a job and moved into your house when I was recovering and then I was afraid to leave, but I'm not anymore."

"Good, that's all good. No need to be mad at me. I just want what's best for you and I know how to—"

"No, Dad. You do not. I quit. I'm not working at Reynolds Construction anymore and I'm going to speed up the timetable for moving out of your house."

"It's not a good idea to quit one job without having another one lined up," her dad said.

"It's not your concern, Dad. I'm taking back my life and I'll make my own decisions from now on."

Harrison shook his head. "Damn stubborn girl. Talk to her, Chris."

"Macy," he said.

But his betrayal hurt worse than her dad's and she held her hand up to him. "I can't talk to you right now, Chris."

"Honey, you are overreacting," he said.

She knew she wasn't. She'd wanted to believe in him, but the truth was, she was only seeing what she wanted to see, not the real man. "I am not overreacting, Chris. I think if you heard your mom and I making a deal for you, you'd be outraged. Why do you men think you can go behind my back and make plans for my life?"

"We don't think that," Chris said.

"Then why are you having a cozy little drink with my dad and saying you're going to ask me to marry you?" she demanded.

"Because I want you to be my wife," Chris said. "I'd think that's obvious. And I know you want to be too because you're not the kind of woman who can be intimate with a man and not want to be married to him," Chris said, leaning forward so that only she heard what he said.

She gasped and took a huge step away from him before she slapped him. How dare he! "I can't believe you just said that to me. I don't want to discuss this anymore. Have dinner with my dad and work on your little plan to make sure you both get the club development deal, but that's all you are getting in Royal, Texas, Christopher Richardson, because I'm not a bargaining chip for either of you to use."

She turned on her heel and stomped out of the club. As soon as she was outside she almost collapsed. She was tired, angry and so hurt she wanted to curl up in a ball and die. But she couldn't—not yet.

She heard the door open behind her. She turned, hoping it would be Chris, but it was a dark-haired man she didn't know.

She walked to her car and got in it. Once she started driving, she had no idea where to go and ended up at a hotel near the highway. She checked in and sat on the bed trying not to cry.

As bad as her car accident had been, she'd never felt this broken on the inside. Her looks could be fixed. Her bones healed and her scars would eventually fade. But this wound on her heart was going to be there for a very long time. She'd never recover from the pain that Chris had given her when he'd bargained with her father for a slice of his business and an opportunity to be a part of the Texas Cattleman's Club in exchange for marrying her.

She rolled onto her side, hugging the pillow close, and let the tears fall. No one was here to see the weakness, so she let her broken heart and her tears fill her for the night. Tomorrow she'd make plans and get ready to move on.

But just lying on the bed crying wasn't good enough for her. She had been through so much pain that wallowing in it didn't suit her at all.

She needed a plan of action. Something to give her focus. She'd have the movers get her stuff from her father's house tomorrow and then she'd call her old boss at Starwood. It was an international company—there had to be positions that would get her out of Royal. Because she thought it was time to leave.

That was the only way her father was going to understand she was serious and that she wasn't going to let anyone use her.

She reached for the notepad on the bedside table and started making a list. Lists appealed to her, so she jotted down a few things, but then her mind turned to Chris. Why couldn't he have just asked her to marry him?

She wouldn't have even minded if later on he tried to finagle some sort of deal with her dad as long as he'd asked her to marry him first.

That wasn't true. She wanted him to love her the way

she loved him and she knew she'd never do anything to hurt Chris even after he'd made her this mad. She wanted to make herself fall out of love with him, but this time she hadn't had a schoolgirl crush on him and it was going to take a lot of time to heal this wound.

Two days later Macy still wouldn't return any of his calls and Chris was left with a major decision. He could either stay in the running to do the development project and have Macy think that was more important to him than she was, or drop out and then figure out how to get her back.

It was surprisingly one of the easiest decisions he'd ever had to make. He picked up his phone and called Brad.

"It's Chris," he said when Brad answered. "I'm going to have to withdraw my name from consideration for doing the development at the club."

"Why? What happened?" Brad asked.

"I have too many commitments," Chris said. And he had a big one he was planning to make with Macy. She was the only thing that mattered. He'd known that when they'd made love at the swimming hole. He should have told her how he felt then.

"Is there anything I can say to change your mind?" Brad asked.

"No, I'm sorry. But Floyd seems like he'll do a good job for you."

"He does, but Abby found him."

"She will never let you forget it either," Chris said.

"Tell me about it. Thanks for the call," Brad said before hanging up.

Chris had to make some decisions about his future

and he needed a plan to get Macy back. He had to clear the air with Harrison. He called the older man and got his voice mail. "This is Chris Richardson. I'd like to talk to you. Call me at my office."

Then he called the florist and ordered a dozen roses to be sent to Macy. He knew she was living in her old house now because…well, he'd driven by there last night. And he'd seen her through the window. He'd felt like a creepy stalker, so he hadn't gone to her door.

He didn't want to screw up with her again. The next time they met face-to-face he was going to get her to agree to be his wife and then they'd never be apart again. He could do that, just barely.

He tried to work, but wanted to talk to Harrison. Nothing was going to be okay in his life until he had Macy back by his side. It had been six hours since he'd left his message for Harrison, so he called again and finally got through. Macy's dad agreed to meet him at his office.

Tanja knocked on his door just as he hung up. "Um…a floral-delivery guy just dropped off a dozen roses… He said that the lady who you sent them to refused them."

"Dammit."

"Sorry, Chris. Is there anything I can do?" Tanja asked.

"You can take the roses home," he said. "I'm expecting Harrison Reynolds. Show him in as soon as he gets here."

Chris figured if he had Macy on his home turf he'd have a better chance of winning her over. So he started making plans in his head. He'd have his private plane— no, that wouldn't work—she wouldn't get on his plane if he sent it for her. He'd have to find a plane and then get her to Dallas. He'd have her brought to him and then—what? He'd pour his heart out.

"I'm here. What did you want?" Harrison said as he let himself into the office. The door closed firmly behind him.

"We need to talk and I'm not taking any chances of anyone overhearing what I have to say."

"Fair enough, I owe you at least that. Have you heard from Macy?"

"No," Chris said. "I guess she was good to her word about quitting."

"Hell, yes. She moved out too. Did it while I was at work," Harrison said.

"She's at her old house," Chris said.

"I know," Harrison said. "I sent one of my guys by yesterday to check on her and she sent him back with a mouthful for me."

Chris had to chuckle. Macy was a spitfire and she was his and he wanted her back. "I love your daughter, Harrison, and I'm going to do whatever I have to in order to get her back. I already withdrew from the Texas Cattleman's Club development."

"I figured you would. You don't really need the business," Harrison said.

"Well, no business deal is worth more to me than Macy is and I aim to prove that to her."

"Good. I'm sorry I pushed so hard for the merger the other day. I just…Macy's all I've got and I want the company to be an inheritance for her and her kids. And I know if I let it go to someone who isn't related, it wouldn't be as prosperous as it would be in your hands."

"Thank you for that. We can discuss it after Macy and I have been married at least five years."

Harrison chuckled at that. "I don't think so."

"Harrison," Chris said, leaning forward so the older man would understand how serious he was. "You had better understand that Macy is my one chance at happiness. You ruined it for me once. I'm not going to let you do that again."

"I get that, boy."

"Don't call me boy. I'm not some oil rigger's son anymore. I'm definitely your peer and I am going to be your son-in-law. If we have to have an uneasy truce, that's fine with me, but I'm hoping you will want more than that."

Harrison sat back in his chair studying Chris. "What are you going to do?"

"I'm going to head back to Dallas and then convince her to come back to me. I can't fight for her in Royal. We have too many gossips and all that old history here. I want to start fresh."

"Good. I want to be there. Not when you ask her to marry you, but the next day. Macy's all I've got left in this world and I don't like not seeing and talking to her."

Chris understood that. His mother was the same way. "Okay, will you bring my mom to Dallas with you? We can all have breakfast when she agrees to marry me."

"*If* she agrees," Harrison said.

"I'm banking on the fact that I've only hurt her. Hurt I can make up for. If I've made her stop loving me…"

"I don't think you have," Harrison said. "Did you see the way she yelled at me? I was the one she took most of her anger out on. I think she didn't want to say anything to you she'd regret."

"I hope so," Chris said. But he knew he deserved her anger. Given the situation with Harrison from their

youth, Chris should never have been talking to him
without Macy by his side. She'd been unsure of him
from the beginning.

"I need someone who she will listen to," Chris said,
talking more to himself.

"You need Abigail Langley. Macy trusts her. They've
been good friends through some dark times. I think
she's the one who will be your best bet," Harrison said.

"She hates me," Chris said.

"She doesn't hate me. Let me call her and see what
we can do," Harrison said.

"Why are you helping me?" Chris asked.

"I misjudged you, and I have never seen Macy
happier than she's been these past few weeks. I know
you'll find a way to win her back and I want to be part
of it."

"Why?"

"Because you're going to be the father of my grand-
children and I'm going to want to see them."

Chris had a chuckle at that. He was determined to
win Macy back, but he was far from sure that he could
do it as easily as Harrison seemed to think he could.
Chris sat back in his chair ready to put in as many hours
as he had to in order to get Macy back.

Macy turned another florist away—this was the
fourth one in as many days—and went back to work
in her home office. She was still mad. Once she'd
decided that crying wasn't part of the solution, she'd
been energized working on her to-do list. The list gave
her something to focus on instead of missing Chris.
And she did miss him.

She couldn't sleep at night because she woke up

dreaming of him. That was the hardest time. During the day she made calls for jobs—her lead at Starwood had fallen through—and worked with the hospital on setting up their next fashion show, which would take place in December. Maggie Richardson's friend Norma from the hospital had been a godsend.

Macy hadn't gone to see Maggie, not wanting to run into Chris. But she was going to have to approve Maggie's new clothing designs sometime this week. She checked her watch and figured that Chris would still be at work at this time of day.

She hopped into her car and made the quick drive across town. Maggie answered the door with a big smile on her face.

"Hello, Macy. I'm so glad you could come over today," she said.

"Me too. Let me see those sketches. I want to get out of here before Chris comes home," Macy said.

"Oh, he's gone back to Dallas," Maggie said. "I thought, well, I thought that was why you came over today."

"I didn't know. What about his work at the club?"

"He withdrew his name, said he was too busy," Maggie said.

Macy didn't know what to say or how to act. She had a million questions, but since she'd refused to answer any of his calls, she didn't think it would be fair to grill his mom about why he'd turned down the business and left Royal.

"I'll go get the sketches for you to approve," Maggie said.

Macy was left alone in the living room and she drifted over to the window to glance out at the backyard.

She was confused. She'd been keeping busy until…until what? She didn't know, but a part of her had hoped that maybe he'd come and beg her forgiveness.

But all those flowers she'd returned must have sent the message that she never wanted to talk to him again. That hadn't been her intent. What *was* her intent? Knowing he'd left cooled her anger. Now she wanted to talk to him. But it was too late. He'd moved on and once again left her behind in Royal.

"Here they are," Maggie said, coming back into the room. Macy took the sketches to the dining room table and spread them out. Since the event would take place in December they were doing a Christmas theme and she looked at the little elf costumes for the boys and girls and wanted to smile.

"Why did he just leave like that?" Macy asked.

"I don't know. He did say he'd be back for the Christmas show."

She didn't want to have to wait until December to see him, but she'd have to. Unless she accepted his flowers. But she wanted more of an apology than a bouquet of roses. He'd really hurt her.

"These are fine, Maggie," Macy said. "I'd love to stay and chat a little more, but I've got another meeting at the hospital." She left a few minutes later and got in her car and just sat there. Chris had left Royal without telling her? What had she expected?

How was she going to make her to-do list keep her from calling Chris? Keep her from trying to figure out if he still wanted her or if he'd given up on her altogether?

She pulled her cell phone from her purse. She unlocked it and hit the pictures icon. There was the photo of her and Chris. The one time they'd made love and it had been glorious. They both looked happy there.

How had things gotten to this point? Had she jumped to conclusions? Should she go and talk to her dad?

"Ugh," she said, leaning forward to rest her head on the steering wheel.

She put the car in drive, and her phone rang as she pulled back into her driveway. It was Abby.

"Hey. What's up?"

"I need your help with the flamingos again."

The last time the flamingos had been moved, it was to the club, and she and Chris had their first kiss right in front of the flock. She felt a sting of tears.

"I can't."

"I haven't even told you when we are doing them," Abby said.

"Chris went back to Dallas."

"Oh, man, you're kidding me. I thought he was still sending you flowers every day," Abby said.

"He is, but I guess today might have been the last time. I don't know what to do."

"Well, getting out of your house might help," Abby said.

"We kissed in front of the flamingos, I just can't help you do them," Macy said.

"Fair enough. Let me think about it and I will call you back."

Macy hung up the phone and went into her house. It was only as she closed the door behind her that she realized she was retreating from the world the way she had when she'd had her accident. Today was the first day she'd left the house since she'd quit her job with her father and told Chris she wouldn't marry him to sweeten a business deal.

She'd turned back into the same woman she'd been before Chris had arrived in Royal. She suspected that if she hadn't run into Chris that day in the hospital she would have just gone back to her routine of not socializing and hiding away from the world.

She didn't want to be that person. She liked getting out. She'd been looking forward to going to the Royal High School Cheerleaders Gabfest, but then had canceled because of Chris. She had to figure out how to live her life.

And she also had to decide if she wanted Chris in her life. She leaned forward and looked in the hall mirror. She had a new face and a body that was fully recovered. Had she worked that hard only to walk away from love?

"Hell, no," she said to her reflection.

She needed a plan and a new to-do list. A list that would get her the one thing she truly wanted—and that was the man she loved as her husband.

Chris was going to learn that if he made her mad they'd fight it out, but he had to stop running away and she had to stop hiding. That was the first thing she'd say to him after she hugged him and told him she loved him.

Now she just had to figure out how to find him in Dallas. She figured she could get Maggie's help if she told the older woman how much she loved Chris.

Thirteen

"There is a call for you from Abigail Langley. She said it's urgent and she must speak with you today," Bettina said. Bettina was Chris's administrative assistant in Dallas.

"Put her through," Chris said. He turned his chair so that he could see downtown Dallas. The city had been home to him for most of his adult life and yet this week he'd felt lost here. Adrift because he didn't know how to get through to Macy. Now he had this one chance to convince Abby to help him.

"This is Chris," he said into the speaker phone. She had to at least be happy that he was out of the running for the Texas Cattleman's Club's new development. Having her man get the job would give her an edge over Brad.

"It's Abby Langley. Harrison said you wanted to talk to me," she said.

"That was three days ago," Chris said. As soon as he said, it he regretted it, but he was tired of waiting to get Macy back and she hadn't returned any of his calls or accepted one bouquet of flowers he'd sent.

"Do you still need me?" she asked, sounding very impatient.

More than he wanted her to know. If he could have figured out how to get Macy back on his own, he'd already have her in his arms, but he needed help to do this. "Yes, I do. I want Macy back and she won't take my calls."

"I don't blame her. Women shouldn't be bartered," Abby said.

Chris was tired of being blamed for something that wasn't entirely his fault. He hadn't bartered for Macy and he never would. He wanted her so badly that he'd pay any price to have her back.

"You should get your facts straight. That wasn't the situation," Chris said.

"Well, that's what Macy thinks. What do you need me to do?" she asked.

Chris had the feeling that if he didn't say the right thing Abby would hang up on him. And as much as that irritated him, it also made him glad that Macy had a friend like Abby who not only had her back but would go to bat for her.

"Can you bring her to Dallas? She won't come for her dad or me, but I thought maybe you could suggest a girls' trip. I'll pay for everything." He'd give up his entire fortune. All the money he'd worked so hard for and saved like a miser to prove to the people of Royal that he was a success—he'd give it all up for her.

"If I do this for you, you will owe me a favor,"

Abby said. He could almost hear the gears turning as she thought of the way to work this situation to her advantage.

"What kind of favor?" he asked.

"Your expertise on Floyd Waters's development efforts," she said.

"Okay, but you do everything the way I ask for it to be done," Chris said. He could handle giving advice to Waters. The man was a solid developer and with some more experience would probably be giving Chris a run for his money. But Macy was something different. He didn't want Abby going off on her own plan. Everything had to be the way he wanted it.

"What do you have in mind?"

"Do you have a plane?"

"Yes. So I'm bringing her to Dallas?"

"She'd be suspicious if she saw my plane."

"Agreed. Why are we coming to Dallas again?" Abby asked.

"Girls' weekend."

"Great, but once you scoop her up what am I going to do?" Abby asked.

"Go back to Royal and continue your campaign to become the next president of the Texas Cattleman's Club."

She laughed. "Why should I help you with this? Are you going to promise to never hurt her again?"

Chris had done little else but think about that very thing for the past four days. "I love her, Abby."

"Do you really?"

"Yes. Would I be begging you for help if I didn't? I could leave Royal and never look back but I can't—won't—leave Macy behind. She's too important to me."

"Promise me you won't hurt her, Chris," Abby said.

"I'd rather die than hurt her again," Chris admitted.

"That's good enough for me," she said after a pause.

"Okay… Thanks… I need you to bring her to Knox Street on Friday. You can say you are going shopping and I will surprise her there. Which store will you go to first?"

"I…I think Pottery Barn. She's just moved back into her house and she needs some stuff for it."

"I'll be there. Can you text me when you land?"

"I will," Abby said. "If she doesn't want to see you, Chris, I'm going to take her back on the plane."

"Fair enough. If she doesn't want me then I will bow out of her life. I want her to be happy and smiling, not hurt because of anything I've done or that she thinks I've done."

"You're a good man, Chris."

"I try," he said and hung up the phone.

He stood up and left his office. "I'm going out for the rest of the afternoon," he said to Bettina on his way out.

He headed downtown to Knox Street and checked out the location where she'd be. There was a big parking lot in the back of Pottery Barn and for the right price Chris was able to secure half of it for Friday afternoon.

He knew everything hinged on his plan. He wanted the right band to be playing and enough flowers to make her think she'd stumbled into the Garden of Eden. He walked up and down Knox Street finding all the right vendors and getting everything set up.

He had to wait two more days to see her again and he wasn't too sure he could do it. So he holed up in his office and started working on the plans for his dream home. Every room he added he imagined Macy in it. He thought about her home in Royal and put in touches of the things that he knew she liked.

It made him feel closer to her doing this. He continued working on the plans day and night until it was Friday morning. He took extra time with his appearance and when he got the text from Abby saying they were landing in Dallas he wiped his sweaty palms on his pants and got in his Porsche.

He drove to Knox Street and waited, hoping that this time when he saw Macy he'd be able to give her the ring he had in his pocket and that she'd say yes to being his wife.

He didn't know if he'd be able to let her go if she didn't say yes. He almost forgot to breathe when he saw the limo pull into the parking lot and then the door opened.

Macy had been more than happy to accept Abby's invitation to come to Dallas. She wanted to be closer to Chris. The flowers had stopped the day she'd found out he'd left Royal, and she had his business address, so she figured while she was here, she'd call him and see if they could talk. She was more than ready to start over with him.

"I'm so glad we can finally come to Dallas to celebrate your recovery."

"Me too," Macy said. "And your suggestion that I buy things for the house was a good one. I need to redo all the rooms. They feel stagnant, as if they are part of my old life."

"I bet they do," Abby said. "After Richard died the house still felt like him. I can't really explain it."

Macy reached across the seat to squeeze her friend's hand. "I understand what you mean. We both need this weekend away. I'm glad you could take a break from campaigning."

"I had a minor victory when Chris withdrew his name," Abby said with a smile.

"Yay!" She was happy for her friend, even though Abby's victory at the Texas Cattleman's Club had directly led to her not knowing where Chris was exactly. Not that she in any way blamed Abby.

"Where are we staying?" Macy asked. She hadn't asked many questions, since Abby's offer to fly them to Dallas for a shopping trip seemed the solution she'd been searching for.

"It's a surprise," Abby said.

The flight was quick and soon they were on the ground and in the limo. "My dad used to bring me here to go back-to-school shopping."

"I remember. He has always doted on you," Abby said.

"Yes, he has. It's been hard not talking to him, but I want him to realize he can't keep playing around with my life."

Abby nodded. "You made the right decision. So when are you going to forgive him?"

"I think I already have. We're all each other has and knowing that he's only looking out for me...well, to be honest, I don't know what he was thinking to try to use his business to schmooze Chris."

Macy had been over that situation in her head several times and no matter how hard she tried she just couldn't figure out why her dad had done that. He was the kind of man who'd never let go of his company to anyone.

The limo pulled to a stop and the driver came around to open the door. Abby gestured for Macy to get out first and she got out and stopped in her tracks. Chris stood in front of her wearing a tux.

A band started playing "You're Beautiful." The lead singer sounded similar enough to James Blunt that she stopped to double-check it wasn't him.

Chris walked over to her holding out his arms. She hesitated, but Abby got out of the car behind her and nudged her toward Chris. "You know you want to go to him."

"I do," she said.

Chris pulled her into his arms. "I would sacrifice anything for you, Macy. You are the true prize of my life and without you I have nothing."

She held him close.

"I love you so much," he said.

"I love you too, Chris. More than I thought I could."

Chris got down on one knee while the band continued to play and took a black velvet box from his pocket. He held it in one hand and opened it. She caught a sparkling glint off the stone before he took her hand in his.

"Macy Reynolds, I fell for you the first time you flashed me that sexy little smile of yours and I was a fool to let you go when I was eighteen. Please let me make up for the years we lost by spending the rest of our lives together."

"Christopher Richardson, there is nothing I want more than to be your wife and spend the rest of my life by your side."

Chris let out a loud whoop of joy and put the ring on her finger. She didn't even have a chance to look at it before he was kissing her and lifting her in his arms and spinning her around.

"We're never going to be apart again," he said.

"That suits me perfectly," she said.

The next morning Chris woke her with a kiss on the lips. "Good morning, my beautiful fiancée."

"Good morning to you, husband-to-be," she said. She'd had time to admire the ring yesterday afternoon and it was exquisite. Even Abby had agreed. She'd stayed for dinner with them but then had gone back to Royal.

"What are our plans for today?" she asked, rolling over on her side so that the sheets fell off her and bared her breasts to his gaze.

"Breakfast and then how about a little venue research," he said, reaching out to cup her breasts in his hands.

"You want to get married in Dallas? I kind of wanted it to be in Royal," she said.

"If that's what you want then we will do it there. Maybe on your father's ranch?"

"Yes, but I think I have to call him and smooth things over with him first."

"We can do that after breakfast," he said, kissing her soundly.

Macy was never going to get used to waking up next to him. She was so happy that Chris had come back to Royal and they'd had this second chance at love. The real tragedy in her life would have been missing out on this.

They made love in the shower and then got dressed. When they got downstairs, Macy saw that Chris's housekeeper had set up a breakfast buffet on the patio and when she stepped out back by the pool she saw why.

"Dad?"

"Hello, Macy. I hope you don't mind, but I wanted to be here to say congratulations and to ask you to forgive me for trying to toy with your life."

Her dad looked tired and worried. She went over to him and gave him a hug. "Of course I forgive you. I know you were only concerned for me."

"And for your future," he said. "Chris has the ability to keep Reynolds Construction going strong long after I'm gone, but I'm not pushing for that anymore. This is about you and him now."

She kissed his cheek, realizing that her dad wasn't going to stop pushing for what he wanted and she knew now that Chris loved her and didn't need anything else in his life to be happy.

"Thank you, Daddy. I'm so glad you are here this morning."

"Me too," he said, giving her one of his big bear hugs that made her feel wrapped up in his love.

Maggie walked out on the patio next and Macy went over and gave Chris's mom a kiss. She looked happy this morning as she lifted Macy's hand to look at her engagement ring.

"I'm so glad you two resolved your problems. I didn't like it when you were split up."

"Me neither," Chris said.

"Me neither," Macy said at the same time.

He twined their hands together and led the way to the table for breakfast. They spent the morning talking about their plans for the future and Macy knew she'd found more than she'd ever expected to when she found

Chris. She'd found love and the promise of a future that had everything she'd ever dreamed of.

Chris lifted her hand to his mouth and kissed the back of it.

"What are you thinking about?" he asked.

"How great our future is going to be," she said.

"It is going to be great," Chris agreed. "And we have a great story to tell our kids about how Grandpa tried to break us up, but we didn't let him."

"You might not want to tell that story, Chris," Harrison said.

"Why not?"

"What if you end up with a headstrong girl like Macy? She'll be running wild with all kinds of boys and telling you that you are acting like me if you try to stop her," Harrison said with a big laugh.

Chris shook his head. He looked forward to having a girl with Macy's pretty eyes and features who'd make him crazy as long as she had. With Macy by his side he could do anything and would be very happy.

"Are you two planning to settle down in Royal?" Harrison asked.

"We haven't really had a chance to discuss that, but I'd like to divide our time between Dallas and Royal," Chris said.

"I like that idea," Macy added.

"Me too," said Maggie.

"We can still do business together," Harrison added. "Now that we've cleared up our misunderstanding—"

"Misunderstanding? My company didn't do anything wrong. You consistently bid higher than everyone else," Chris said goodnaturedly.

"You get what you pay for in the building business,"

Harrison said. "But now that you and Macy are settling down I might give you a family discount."

Macy couldn't help but laugh at the way her father said that. She suspected that despite the respect he and Chris held for each other they'd continue to butt heads.

She didn't let that bother her. Everything that Chris did seemed to please Macy, and they both looked forward to a life of happiness and love and laughter together.

* * * * *

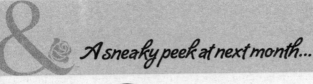

A sneaky peek at next month...

Desire™

PASSIONATE AND DRAMATIC LOVE STORIES

2 stories in each book - only £5.49!

My wish list for next month's titles...

In stores from 16th March 2012:

☐ Enticed by His Forgotten Lover – Maya Banks

& The Billionaire's Borrowed Baby – Janice Maynard

☐ Reclaiming His Pregnant Widow – Tessa Radley

& To Touch a Sheikh – Olivia Gates

☐ An After-Hours Affair – Barbara Dunlop

& Millionaire Playboy, Maverick Heiress – Robyn Grady

☐ Much More Than a Mistress – Michelle Celmer

& Bachelor Untamed – Brenda Jackson

Available at WHSmith, Tesco, Asda, Eason, Amazon and Apple

Just can't wait?

Visit us Online

You can buy our books online a month before they hit the shops! **www.millsandboon.co.uk**

0312/51

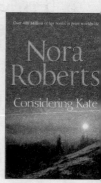

The World of Mills & Boon®

There's a Mills & Boon® series that's perfect for you. We publish ten series and with new titles every month, you never have to wait long for your favourite to come along.

Blaze.   Scorching hot, sexy reads

By Request   Relive the romance with the best of the best

Cherish   Romance to melt the heart every time

Desire   Passionate and dramatic love stories

Visit us Online   Browse our books before you buy online at **www.millsandboon.co.uk**

M&B/WORL

Have Your Say

You've just finished your book.
So what did you think?

We'd love to hear your thoughts on our
'Have your say' online panel
www.millsandboon.co.uk/haveyoursa

- 🌹 Easy to use
- 🌹 Short questionnaire
- 🌹 Chance to win Mills & Boon® goodies